DiaRy
of a
HeReTic

A NOVEL

by

Kathleen Maher

BEEKMAN PRESS
New York, NY 10038

TABLE OF CONTENTS

The Paragon of Level-Headedness
In Any Furious Moment
No Eye Contact, Please
I Remember
One Hundred Percent Used-to-Be
We Couldn't Have Held On
Plan B
Faith Like Desire

To Manny

PART ONE: The Beginning of the End

Justifying My Existence

For years I adhered to the idea that if I lived spartanly and maintained hope, a day would come when I would be invited to speak my mind. And someone would listen. Someone would understand.

I imagined an intimate gathering of sympathetic souls: When you were called upon to speak, you'd be encouraged to say why you're alive, why you were born, and why you're still around: What are your reasons?

Everyone would have to come up with an answer. After all, no one gets through life without having to justify their existence.

The problem is that there's so much stuff we don't know how to express. Whenever I ask someone: "Does it ever strike you how weird, how really extreme it is, being a person, this thing, yourself?" Generally, people say, "What are you talking about?"

Oh, occasionally someone quick, someone who was actually listening, will say: "Well, maybe it is weird being *you*, Malcolm."

A response that's lighthearted and clever, but ducks the question. As if it's gauche to ask, let alone answer: "Why am I alive? What's the point?"

People hate to admit their ignorance. They would rather cling to faiths or theories that are, in fact, very hard to believe, but for them, I guess, easier than saying, "Duh? I don't know," their whole lives.

Personally, I think that special people, who work at it constantly, do get a clue. But they are so rare and their hard-won intimation so cryptic everyone else thinks they're crazy.

Perhaps the best you can do is: ignore the odds. Hope and pray that the impetus behind your actions glides along an invisible, parallel course exerting a distinct pull. Grasp it and you'll have an answer. ≈

Double Fantasy

January 1

Was it a joke? Was he reading my diary? After closing our little café yesterday evening, after all the money was counted and our customers had gone home to prepare for whatever New Year's Eve rituals they would endure or enjoy, my head baker, the impossible, arrogant Carlos Villalobos, produced a bottle of Taittinger champagne and two tulip-shaped glasses. Carlos works hard to project a sinister air, with his weathered, houndish face and dyed-brown braid to his waist, but he suddenly dropped the act. "To the New Year!" he said.

Feeling loose and flushed, I sat on the countertop. Carlos and I have worked together for six years. And though we have an uneasy relationship, he does know me. He knows I'm socially out of practice. I almost never leave this little brick building in our drowsy suburb at the last stop of Chicago's elevated train system. I work all day in the shop and sleep upstairs, and my excursions are limited to supply runs.

So I honestly don't know: Do people describe their pet fantasies the way they talk about the weather? Is it socially acceptable to talk about your fondest, impossible dream, the one you know will never happen, even though it won't let go of you? To which a new-found friend might say, "Nice dream. Here's mine…"?

Mildly giddy, I told Carlos that someday I want to start a discussion group where people say all the stuff no one dares to think about in private, "let alone," I said, "describe out loud!"

Impassive, inscrutable Carlos suddenly dropped all pretense; he grabbed my arm and pulled me close. "That's a great idea!"

His enthusiasm startled me, and I squirmed, trying to laugh it off. But Carlos pressed for more and I couldn't help elaborating. I told him how I rely on this fantasy to lift me from my darkest moods. It's not exactly impossible, by any means. I do have the site already established here. What if our little coffee shop shed its sleepy ambience and became a meeting place for like-minded souls; a haven for psychological and emotional troubles; where you were free to share the details, the ins and outs, the maybes and what-ifs surrounding our most urgent lifelong desires; our reasons for living, if you will?

Then I remembered my manners and asked him, "What about you? What do you want to happen in the New Year?"

Carlos planted a hand on either side of my thighs and smirked. "You'll never believe it."

"Yes I will."

"I want the same as you," Carlos said. "And I want it this year."

"With me, it's just something I dream about, but not in any real context."

"Name one reason we can't do it," Carlos said.

"It's my private fantasy. Actually starting it, if it were possible, would change everything."

Carlos refilled our glasses. "Everything's changing anyway. I've watched you a long time, Malcolm, and I can tell: You can do it. And with me orchestrating, it could make money."

I laughed and the worst of my fear abated. "For a second, I thought you were serious."

He nodded and pointed a long skinny index finger at me.

We finished the whole bottle of champagne. I was surprised so much time had passed. It was almost midnight, the New Year. He wrapped the tulip-shaped glasses in two dishtowels and set them carefully in his backpack. When he put on his wool cap, I blurted out, "Hey, you're not going. Look at the clock. Ten minutes."

"Don't be ridiculous." He zipped up his thick leather jacket.

"If you leave before twelve, you're being—stingy."

"Malcolm, all these years? It's too late for you to get sentimental." Kissing my cheeks, he said, *"Próspero Año Nuevo!"* and left me alone in the shop. ≈

Show Time

Yesterday at about six o'clock, when I got back from my flour supplier, I saw a large vinyl sign flapping across the plate-glass window of our shop, announcing the first "Open Mike Night"—tonight! And beneath that, my topic:

HOW CAN WE KNOW ANYTHING
IF WE ONLY BELIEVE WHAT
WE WANT TO BELIEVE?

Apparently, while drinking the New Year's champagne, I had divulged my opening topic to Carlos. I remember drinking and talking. About the topic, I remember him frowning. But he must have decided he liked it, despite himself. For Carlos has seen and done everything three times over, something he never lets me forget. He's worked in every ashram and monastery between LA and San Francisco. He's studied religion his entire life and considers himself an authority.

Nonetheless, the set-up astounded me. The sign! The

banner! It was terrifying. About the topic, I pretended nonchalance, in my too-intense way. But Carlos motioned me toward the swinging door to the kitchen.

"Our timing's dead on. See how the shop's filling up?"

I saw old Mr. Downey and old Mr. Hedlund, who, it's true, normally leave by five. They come every day at three-thirty, drink espresso, eat biscotti and pay twenty percent of their bill —their reading of the seniors' twenty-percent discount I offer. Unfailingly, I explain the math on their receipts, but the old men—eyes, I swear, twinkling—turn off their hearing aids until I give in and shout, "After you drive me out of business, *then* what are you going to do?"

It was out of the norm that the old guys were still sitting there, but downright surreal when a group of supposed graduate students entered and sat down. They whispered as if waiting for a performance, when really *they* were the performance.

"Obvious shills," I hissed at Carlos. But he grinned at me and turned. His nice little butt kept shifting oh-so-close to me. Meanwhile an *influx* of academic types kept our front door bell tinkling.

"Ready, Malcolm?" Pulling off his hair net, Carlos crossed the kitchen, his braid swinging from side to side. From my office, he dragged out a microphone.

"Are you crazy?" I waved my arms. "The room's way too small for that."

Laying his hands on my shoulders, he put his mouth near my ear, "Don't worry."

Once he set up the mike, I figured: It's my shop, my dream, *I'm* doing the sound check!

"Testing, testing…" And, sure enough, my voice was so loud, everybody winced.

Bounding back over, Carlos readjusted the apparatus, and, embarrassingly off key, sang a few phrases from a John Lennon song, the one about life being what happens while you're making other plans. Marking a line on the floor with tape, he said, "Stand here."

"You're making too much of this." I bent over to suppress a choking impulse.

Stephanie, my irritable but highly competent waitress, glared at me as I pressed a fist into my diaphragm, trying to breathe. "Shit, Malcolm, if you're not going to get the cocoas for table three, keep your fat ass out of my way."

Whereupon Carlos, who for six years has categorically refused to serve people, said, "Allow me." He got cocoas and teaspoons, little plates of butter, iced water, and hazelnut cappuccinos.

"It's not funny, Carlos."

"Don't be stupid. I've seen these things happen before. But never with so much potential."

I groaned and Carlos said, "You should decide what you want to be called. How about, 'The World's Most Pink-Skinned Saint?'"

"How much are you paying these out-of-work actors?"

"One rule," Carlos gripped my arm and hissed, "whatever you make the *big* sin—money, sex, ambition—will pervade your religion. Law of nature, Malcolm: the thing you try hardest to overcome will end up corrupting you and all your followers."

"I'm not starting a *religion!* And I don't want followers!" My eyelids burned. "I only want a discussion group—a real one."

"Call it what you want," he said, drawing a knuckle down my left side. Making the walls shift, my hair prickle, my tongue slide over my lips.

"Don't touch me!"

And twisting the ends of his mustache, Carlos patted my cheeks, saying, "Show time, Daddy! Show time."

The café was half-full: old men, students and professors— and Carlos leaned on the wall behind me, near the rest rooms.

Feedback from the microphone concealed the catch in my voice as I opened the meeting. "Welcome everyone to our first open mike night, a discussion group where everyone gets a say. We'll start with a topic but it's open-ended. Follow it or not: *How Can We Know Anything When We Only Believe What We Want to Believe?*"

Everyone stared at me. No one spoke or moved and I had to conquer my panic that this might never pass. I might waver here forever, staring back at these people.

Carlos broke the spell. "Who wants to go first?" he asked, arms folded.

A man and woman stood up, and I hastily added, "The main thing is: No rules. Anyone can talk about anything."

At this point, I suddenly suffered a digestive attack, requiring me to tighten up for all I was worth. Edging toward the rest rooms, I suspected Carlos of deliberately blocking my way. He stuck a thumbs-up in my face.

"If there's a lull," he whispered, letting me pass, "want me to improvise?"

When I returned, a pear-shaped woman in a fitted suit said her name was Connie Llewellyn and, her words reverberating, "We're born with a map, DNA, and anyone of normal intelligence who can't solve the puzzle simply isn't trying."

"Dr. Victor Smith" harrumphed on the sideline and took the mike from his stage-wife. "It doesn't explain why a child has to die, struck by a speeding SUV out of nowhere."

Red-faced, Connie Llewellyn started to shoot back, when a voluptuous blonde woman twisted in her seat, and with one of those voices that really carries, said, "Sorry, but the only reason we believe anything is to make our lives bearable. Consider how unreliable our eyes and ears are, to say nothing of our minds!"

The married couple was now blatantly playing footsie under their table, as if airing philosophical differences was a kind of "talk dirty to me."

"Sometimes," said the blonde, "If you're alert, the truth is beating inside a box in your brain, demanding to be let out."

Tipping back in her chair, she said, "If we don't overload ourselves with busyness, we already know way too much."

Extricating himself from his wife's toe-hold, Victor Smith half-stood. "Re-enroll, Ms. Townsend, and for this alone, I shall give you an A."

Ms. Townsend exhaled in a rush. "Who cares if we matter? I mean, not just ultimately but constantly."

I could not follow what she said next. Two old guys were waving for more pink fructose water, which I grabbed from the case. My perspective as I crossed the room jumped wildly, as if I were watching a series of overwrought camera angles. ≈

Billowing Worry

Carlos convinced me the meeting was basically authentic. "You think I paid them? At most they got a free cupcake. They'll be back. They, along with many others, in time."

Maybe. After all, once the conversation began, it seemed as if no one wanted to stop. What made the meeting worthwhile was the sense of life being such a struggle for everyone, all the time.

So that I convinced myself, "It was perfect, perfect!" Then this afternoon, driving west on Lawrence to my flour supplier, Louie, I got distracted and skipped a beat and the next thing I knew, doubt crept in, changing the refrain to: "Perfect? Come on, Malcolm. Perfect dessert theater."

In front of me was a low-riding station wagon with half a jacket hanging from the trunk. One sleeve was dragging on the ground and the back kept filling with air, forming half a torso and then deflating as the car slowed down. Was our first open discussion group *really* perfect? Or really a waste?

This billowing worry thrummed in my head: *perfect, waste; perfect, waste...*

*

Louie Duvall swore on his mother's grave that the problem with my flour, mealy moths two weeks in a row, was an honest mistake. He threw an arm around me and slipped me an uncovered CD. "All original, man." Louie by night is a blues singer. He yelled into an intercom and a muscle-bound teenager dollied in three 50-pound bags. Louie slit each bag and we leaned over the stuff together to make sure it wasn't infested. Louie's tiny teeth gleamed and the edges of his round little stick-out ears turned translucent. The teenager loaded the bags in my car. Louie pumped my hand and slapped my back and said my next two orders were on the house. The whole visit took less than ten minutes. ≈

Now What?

➢ *Everyone Has Something to Hide.*
➢ *Everyone Wants More.*
➢ *Is Prayer Addicting?*
➢ *Six Ways to Overcome Loneliness.*

That last one sounds good for the second meeting: *Six Ways to Overcome Loneliness.* But what if it attracts a bunch of singles despairing over the big date they can't get. Then what?
≈

Based on Experience

Neither Carlos nor anyone else has ever participated in a fully open discussion group. But my dream comes from real life.

The "College of Complexes" was a group of thinkers and seekers, which disbanded after its meeting place was demolished by bulldozers. Each of its members mysteriously succumbed to whatever fate he or she had been valiantly staving off.

Either that or they bribed the manager at the McDonald's across the street to tell me so, so as to get rid of me.

I discovered the College of Complexes through an ad in a free newspaper's personals, the summer after Colin's death. I was already running the shop and living above it. Staring at a screen, laptop or any type, in those days disgusted me even more than it does now. So when I wasn't working, I read tabloids, poring over the words, repeating them until they became meaningless (when they weren't meaningless to begin with). The notice for the C of C appeared wedged in with ads recalling fantastic, amorous eye contact between strangers.

*To the guy on the Fullerton bus who smiled at me, 7/21, please call
and smile at me again*

Or:

*You, long blond hair, leather jacket. Me, Bulls cap, blue jeans. Too
shy to say hi at the news stand*

I used to study those ludicrous pleas and wonder if the
reason for my ongoing existence—and Colin's nonexistence—
weren't encoded in them. And now it occurs to me that maybe
it was.

I didn't hang around the C of C that much. In two years I
attended several of their meetings—in response to their bold-
faced motto: **Everybody Welcome.** The first meeting to lure
me from my retreat was titled: *Mapping Extreme Terrain: Moral
Ambiguity Amid the Clangor.* The group impressed me as genuine
seeker-martyrs.

In those days, before leaving my apartment, I bathed,
shaved, and followed a rigorous series of self-designed mental
exercises to rid myself of odiousness. And at their meetings, I
only sat in the back and watched.

So why would I wonder if they bribed the counterman at
McDonald's?

Well, for one thing, motto or no motto, the group was
very big on spiritual *quid pro quo:* you were only as holy as you
were poor; enlightenment demanded destitution. With no
exception for someone owning a profitable coffee and pastry
shop (which my parents "invested in" as soon as I dropped out
of college the morning after Colin died.)

I tried to explain myself. Owning a shop, I said, was not

venal in and of itself. I nourished people. For free if need be. And of course *they* were welcome anytime, gratis.

"At a cappuccino place in the suburbs?" asked Hugo, a true seeker-martyr.

"Yes," I said, "but not a far suburb."

Hugo shook his head. "I just don't think so."

For a second there I suspected him of bias against suburbanites: As if, with our driveways and vinyl siding, we deliberately set out to quash transcendence. But then I realized the problem was wholly my own.

If the C of C-ers sweetened their lives with small fictions, so do we all. My problem was how ardently I wanted to be one of them; how desperately I admired them; and that I failed to become intimate with them. ≈

Our Impoverished Souls

The lunch crowd is descending. Stephanie efficiently juggles the table service while I man the takeout and cash register. You'd be surprised how many people want custard-filled coffee cake for lunch, even though we offer three kinds of sandwiches. I double-check the time to see if the beverage truck's coming when I'm seized by the shivers that have been visiting me several times a day, on and off, for weeks. Every hair on my body stands on end and I float back inside with the sense that if I wanted to, I could rise off the floor. I think I can see every molecule in the room: They look like infinitesimal, incandescent sailboats.

Carlos, holding a tray of fresh éclairs, taps me on the shoulder. "Don't go too far, man, you might not get back." A line unfurls in my mind: *Everything that happens has already happened.* From the front comes giggling. Four girls from Northwestern University accompany a rotund character in cape and beret, whose sex I can't tell at first. I look carefully, and decide the character's a he.

The group, tittering, moves to a big table, where they order éclairs and double lattes. The androgynous person brandishes a black cigarette in a shiny gold holder.

I clear my throat. Press my palms together. "I'm afraid there's no smoking."

"No need to soil yourself. I only pretend to smoke."

Two more sets of customers enter and seat themselves. I pour water and retreat to the counter, where I get the lattes going, set the paper doilies on the plates, and begin reaching for the éclairs. Whereupon Carlos's maddening breath once again fills my ear.

"Juice man's here," he whispers. Like it's a big secret. He takes the tongs from me and I stand watching mindlessly as he lays down the last éclair and slyly licks each of his long, sugary fingers. To punctuate the gesture, he grins and looks away. I glimpse his profile—catch and really register it for possibly the first time. There's something naked about it. His eyelids have no lashes. In this light, from this angle, his skin wears a greenish undertone. Is it the light? A new hair dye?

And then: Why didn't I see it before? No wonder his face looks strangely lizard-like. He's shaved off his mustache! But, there he goes, zigzagging from table to table. Carlos the Gila monster, the chameleon, serves the students first, then scurries around, filling orders.

I ought to be grateful.

Carlos is eagerly, efficiently, helping me out. Mr. Raging Superiority is pouring coffee, wiping away crumbs. He's laying out napkins and dispensing miniature jugs of cream, for God's sake! Is this going to be a regular thing?

Until we started the discussion group, Carlos was always the genius and I was the dullard with purse strings. He has ridiculed and berated me since day one because he's the best pastry chef in Chicagoland. On occasion, celebrities extol his confections as their favorite vice.

So I've always put up with a lot of shit from him. But only in the last two weeks has he taken to sidling up to me, casually massaging my shoulders, and whispering, "Relax." His shoulder or forearm is constantly grazing mine. His finger runs along the underside of my arm, and over my chest, under my chin. Twice today, Carlos has placed his firm, dexterous hand at my hip! His heat and energy make me drool. It's all I can do not to curse and shake my fist.

Someone's yelling, "Yo, Malcolm!" from the kitchen when Carlos puts his cold-blooded lips again to my ear. "What did I tell you? Juice man's here."

Bald Paul from Mystic is leaning against the pie shelves, smoking a cigarette like a horn player off his jazz muse, though I happen to know his talents are driving a truck, lifting weights, and believing it's only a matter of time before he wins the lottery. Hairless except for a priapic little black "soul patch" between his mouth and chin, his presence alone embarrasses me. I point to the no smoking poster, and he shrugs. My juice, my coolers, sparkling water, a whole week's worth of milk, cream, and butter are stacked by the walk-in fridge. I glance at the stuff and move my fingers in an attempt to look like speed counting. Then I sign the receipt.

Back at the front tables, the thespians are eating their

gooey éclairs and holding—that is, looking at—the fliers I'd buried in the supply closet, back behind the paper towels, as soon as I'd realized that *Six Ways to Overcome Loneliness* was really a pitiful concept. Takeout customers and those waiting for tables are also holding the fliers, as Carlos announces to the room that the six *ways* of loneliness derive from six *levels*. "Loneliness," he intones, "is the starting point for any and all spiritual awareness."

"Hear, hear," says the person in the cape. Jumping to his feet, raising his cup, he says, "To our impoverished souls! May they grow fat. May they grow bold."

I hurry over to a front table where the dry cleaning man from across the street and Stanley, the pharmacist who works next door, sit looking incredulous.

"What is this?" Stanley asks, a flier in hand.

The dry cleaner, whose name I don't know because unlike R.Ph. Stanley Larson he doesn't wear a name plate, winks. "Getting in on the next big thing, are you?"

Shaking my head, I get them sandwiches. How did Carlos dig up and distribute the fliers so fast? When I return, the dry cleaner wants to know where I am on the six levels to awareness. Four? Five? And are there points in between?

Fool that I am, I say, "Yes, there are points in between."

"So right now, you're trying to surpass what? Four? Four and half?"

"It's hard to say."

"Of course. I shouldn't have asked."

For a second, I wonder if he's making fun of me but when he and Stanley leave, they both ask for fliers to post and hand out in their stores. Apparently, the brilliant Carlos is brilliantly selling his scheme. ≈

Stand and Deliver

January 11

By haranguing me nonstop, Carlos talked me into addressing the issue of loneliness as a spiritual goal. He convinced me "to set the tone" before handing the mike to the first comer. "I know what I'm talking about. You have to be willing to stand up and say what's important."

Because I was afraid to stand up and say what I thought, I knew I must stand up and say it. And yet, acquiescing to him felt like glass cracking, a thin tumbler filling with too hot a liquid—splintering shards and pooling tea.

As the café filled with people I sat in the office, staring at nothing for who knows how long. Eventually I managed to get up and enter the kitchen. No one was there! I was completely alone and so I panicked, I couldn't tell what was just me being psychotic and what might actually have gone awry. Carlos, presumably, was off on some errand, and so his assistants were smoking marijuana in their cars. Closing my eyes, the smells in the room—caramelized pears, chocolate and almond, vanilla cream, sweet yeasty sugar, cinnamon, orange, and cherry kirsch

—invaded my being. The waves of aroma that I smell all day and normally never notice, beckoned with unworldly potency.

Then Carlos materialized at the back door and I jumped, brushing crumbs off my face and chest. Carlos licked his thumb and rubbed a spot on my chin. "Just a smear." My head swiveled as I did a quick inventory. Evidently I'd eaten six brownies. "Looks like—" Carlos patted my stomach, "you put quite a dent in the almond cakes, too." Another swoop, and he pinched me, fore and aft.

"Better drink something to wash it down," Carlos said.

"No, that's okay." But he poured me a tumbler of rich whole milk anyway. Which I glugged without pausing for air.

"How do I look?"

"You look good. You're ready. Don't even think about it," he cooed, his words both cooling and inflaming my neck. He dabbed seductively at my face again, "Go to it, man."

Whereupon I *sailed* to the mike, eyes on a widening horizon. Except—Carlos immediately intervened. Waving his hands, he said, "Excuse me. Excuse me everybody." I cast him a puzzled look and in return, he smirked. "Before we begin," he raised an eyebrow, "I'd like to ask Malcolm—" and he turned to me with a lascivious look, "to talk about worship."

"Worship? We're here to talk about loneliness. Six ways to overcome *loneliness*." I gazed daggers at him.

And in return, Carlos blew me a kiss. The asshole.

"Worship?" I shook my head. "Forget it, Carlos!" And I started to walk out.

But he blocked my path. He held up his hands in an

infuriating—and utterly false—show of innocence. "Why? What's wrong with worship?"

"It's nothing but another master-slave game," I said. "That's what!" I lifted my feet, as if to disentangle myself, but I was already in too deep. "What kind of God," I waved my arms, "demands that his creatures bow down and adulate Him if they want to be anything but lost and miserable their whole lives?"

The reaction to this was a squirming, and then a slow, languid shift. Looking at the faces, I felt a chill. We had the same people as last week attending: the professors, Ms. Maggie Townsend, the blonde, who it turns out is a good friend of Carlos's. Old Mr. Downy and old Mr. Hedlund, and maybe a dozen new faces.

"Um, wait," I sputtered. And before I could stop myself, I was asking if people didn't think an All Knowing, All Powerful God was pretty weird to set things up so His pathetic little creatures must bow and scrape to proclaim His Glory?

"And beyond that, the business of denying our pleasures for the sake of God poses another problem. What if…it's *fun*? What if throwing yourself on the ground and groveling because you're not better than Him feels insanely pleasurable? Does it still count?

"I mean, suppose, contemplating His Wisdom, we rend our clothes. Mortify our flesh. What if we starve ourselves to hear His Voice? Shave our heads and drive toothpicks under our fingernails at the first stirring of sexual sensation—which is what? Constantly? Suppose we practice prayerful, snaking dances, paint our faces and go outside to be despised. If you're like me, you're afraid you might get off on that kind of thing. Does God care if worshipping Him gives us a persistent thrill? Or is it only holy if it hurts?

"And again—you can't get away from this—what if you *like* hurting? Once you've experienced suffering through prayer, even a conservative acknowledgment of God can be enough to trigger euphoria. Whether we wear loincloths or business suits *makes no difference.* Ultimately, the hunger will not go away. The need will not let up!"

*

In the kitchen, Carlos was literally dancing with glee, and I had to grab his elbows to get him to stop. "Why'd you do that to me?"

"I looked at you and the truer issue showed on your face."

"Well, it showed on your face, too! There was a moment," I said, "where everything was going to be okay. Nothing horrible was going to happen, and then your eyes shone with malice."

"It wasn't malice," Carlos said, folding his hands against the small of my back. "Just this once, don't resist."

*

It gets worse. Stephanie and Carlos's friend Maggie Townsend went around collecting unconscionable sums—I'm talking hundreds of dollars!—*in donations.* ≈

Maggie's Mission

January 15

Maggie Townsend is at the shop all the time now. My guess is that Carlos assigned her a secret mission: Hold my hand. Listen to my woes. Cheer me up. Make me smile.

And she's good at it. She's pretty and funny and bops around like a tomboy playing the vamp. Officially, Maggie has started waitressing here, because Stephanie is undependable. Of course, since the second meeting, with the clear smell of money in the air, Stephanie arrives on time. She stays late. In fact, they all hang around, all the time.

At least Maggie is straightforward. To get my attention, she dips and sways and goes into these pretty little yoga stances, clanging invisible chimes. "Don't be so hard on yourself," she says. "'Trix are for kids.'"

"The topic was *loneliness!* Everyone was supposed to stand at the mike. Everyone was to speak his mind. And what happens? Carlos gets me off on the best way to approach God."

"Well I thought you had a point," Maggie says, her hands

suggesting some goddessy maneuver. "Worship like anything else can be a trap."

"Oh Jesus." I lay my head on the table. "I was goaded and tricked and the whole thing is too mortifying to think about it."

"It wasn't that bad," she says. "You're a good speaker and lots of people have never thought about how inherently cheesy traditional worship can be." Maggie smiles for two beats and then breaks into a musical half-scale laugh, a clear alto.

"All right, but what about all that money? Did Carlos put you and Stephanie through some kind of drill?"

"No," Maggie says. "It just happened."

"Yeah, right."

"You didn't do anything wrong," she says.

"What does it matter? My idea for an enlightened group of like-minded souls is finished. It's dead and buried."

"Now *that's* egotistical," Maggie says. "Because you hogged the mike, you're shutting the whole thing down?"

"I'm not! It's Carlos! He's the one who ruined it! It was like I was in a trance. The open mike or discussion group, whatever, is dead! Nothing anyone says or does can resurrect it."

"How come?" Maggie asks.

"Because I hate Carlos. I hate him, I hate him, I hate him."

"Oh," she flashes that crooked little smile, "you think you're the only one?"

"Okay. I hated Carlos before, but that was nothing compared to this. Now I hate him more than anyone! Now I abominate him in every way."

"Which," Maggie says, "is exactly what he was going for."

≈

Revulsion

I have not looked at Carlos once since the meeting. I have not even come close enough to looking at him to know whether he's *noticed* I'm not looking at him.

Oh, I've maintained. Being around him. But it's required tremendous effort. Like walking around with the flu. Just sitting up takes will power, just keeping my eyes open. The need to lie down in a darkened room and let my hatred of him run through me is almost insurmountable. ≈

Further Indignity

I will fire him. Today I held steady even as he slunk around, brushing up against me! His repulsive hand on my shoulder. His long swift fingers alighting at my sides, as he dipped behind me for a knife or slotted spoon. "Excuse me, Slim," his knuckles oh-so-lightly jiggling the extra bit of flesh at my waist.

"Everyone needs to know and say why they're alive." The man had gall!

"You know," he said, his voice a milk-and-honey parody of seduction, "I used to love to talk about my spiritual life. Maybe it was the times, the zeitgeist. When you're young you can say anything. When you're my age, more and more, important things become unpronounceable." ≈

I Have to Admit

Here's his argument (Yes, Carlos is still here. And yes, I *am* going to fire him!): The media constantly informs us of unending war; horrific hi-tech weaponry; mass murders in schools, movie theaters—any place where people form a "mass"—abused children; ritual mayhem; close-ups of greater torture, more brutality, and insurgent, suddenly rampant "brought-in-on-ourselves" diseases. Thus, my little speech about worship far from qualifies as a disaster.

"Every once in a while, Malcolm, you ought to take a peek outside your shell."

Much as I detest him, I have to admit: Even if the man did trick me into calling worship a kind of perversion, even if the whole thing was just as ugly as I think it was—*so what?* My personal humiliation isn't worth mentioning. ≈

How Wrong I Was

Everything's changed!

Carlos and I have spent the last forty-eight hours together. All my senses are heightened and I know: Something good is going to happen. Absolute knowledge gives off a humming sound that intensifies after a while to a constant buzz. Immanent good runs through all my perceptions, waking, sleeping, and in between.

Two days ago, the skies dumped three full feet of snow on city and suburb. And now, forty-eight hours later, the blinding, howling army of snow devils shows no sign of letting up. Cars and trucks cannot make it through. They're lost inside towering drifts.

There is no other news. Life in Chicago has stopped. The CTA is at a standstill. The piercing beeps of plows making minimal progress are incessant.

And—Carlos is with me. That's the main thing, *Carlos is with me!*

Maggie took Saturday off. And Stephanie left hours before

the first flake drifted through the air; she'd heard reports. Carlos, on the other hand chose that static afternoon, a day oppressive with the impending blitz, to experiment with breads. Four new recipes had come to him in a dream.

I started warning him around two-thirty that if he didn't leave he was going to get stuck. (And to think that up until last month he was always gone before noon!)

"Look out the window!" I shouted; snow wasn't so much falling as blasting horizontally past. "You want to get trapped in that? You want to freeze to death?"

He said, "You're too young to remember but it used to snow every winter."

I nodded, yeah, sure, of course it snowed like this all the time. "But didn't you go home before the El froze to a standstill?"

"I wouldn't worry about it." Carlos sprinkled sesame seeds on bread dough.

Fine; get stranded. Carlos should have left an hour ago. Promising to follow his instructions to the letter, promising he could taste the results of his dream-visions tomorrow, providing the plows got through, I handed him his coat and hat.

No dice.

So…He's slept on my couch the last two nights. He's shaved in my sink, bathed in my tub. He has a tattoo on his right shoulder blade, a bluish-green dragon taking flight and breathing fire. Thirty minutes before going to sleep and the same upon waking, he meditates, meaning he sits cross-legged, hands on his knees, palms up, his slow, deep breathing involving an erratic hissing sound.

With the blizzard, Carlos has stopped taunting me. His reptilian gestures against the backdrop of falling snow look more like natural grace than anything calculated. But I've caught myself wondering if this, too, is part of his plan, a way of manipulating me. Except he couldn't have planned how much snow would fall, or for how long.

Clearly my suspicion of Carlos, my distrust and dislike, have been misguided, a reaction to the fact that I've always been so dependent on him as a baker. And then when he usurped my dream of an enlightened discussion group—well, no wonder I hated him!

No more, though. In the sharp glints playing off the brightness of this newly white world I can see how wrong I was. ≈

Stop the Train

January 22

Tonight we ate Spanish rice and drank red wine, which he'd bought during the hushed white afternoon. He went out several times, for a razor, a comb, cumin, green peppers, wine. And returned each time with state-of-the-neighborhood information: Most food and liquor stores were open, but no laundromats or dry cleaners. A group of children tried to coax their German Shepherd to pull their sled. While Carlos waited to buy condoms (because, he explained, militant ascetic though he be, without a fresh handful in his pocket he nonetheless feels in jeopardy), R.Ph. Stan Jenson sold a teenage boy a carton of Camel cigarettes. Maybe he asked for an I.D. card— Carlos didn't see.

Most of the trains ran today; I heard them. Yet Carlos has said nothing of going home. At one point I started to invite him to stay indefinitely, but changed my mind, afraid of scaring him off. These last three days have been so blanketed, so quiet and white and separate; I want them to last forever. ≈

The Hot-Blooded Prophet

January 23

He's washed his socks and underwear in the sink and is drying them in the oven. As I write this, he's padding barefoot in an old robe of mine, his hair unbraided and rippling down his back. He has a set of Chinese iron balls going counter-clockwise in each large thin hand and is pacing the apartment's three rooms, rotating the balls so they chime rhythmically, high and low, without clicking together.

My focus shifts from his fluidly moving fingers and exposed wrists to his tawny feet and surprisingly sturdy ankles. The robe covers his calf muscles and yet I'm so aware of them I have to shut my eyes and swallow hard, which only makes my breath louder and faster. For there is no reflex for blotting out his intense but roving concentration, his flowing hair, and the contrast between the delicate, synchronized chimes in here and the wind outside, which can only hint at the contrast between the callous sunless Carlos I've always known and the magnetism of the hot-blooded prophet circling my floor. ≈

The Invisibles

All through the snow, the shop had a fairly steady string of customers. We fed people who were cold and discouraged after traveling miles on foot and a few who'd flagged a rare bus or train for which they must have waited hours. People dropped into chairs and peeled off layers of sodden clothes. Carlos and I rushed to bring them coffee, tea, hot cider, or cocoa, as they worked their way out of ice-encrusted boots, wrung out wool socks (leaving puddles), asked for pans of warm water and dish towels, anything to warm and then dry their bloodless, sometimes swollen, sometimes frostbitten, feet.

We did not serve donuts. No sticky, gooey non-nutrition: The blizzard people got dark, nutty breads. Since Saturday, when Carlos's dream recipes resulted in four incredible loaves, fragrant with different grains, we've served warm half-loaves with little pots of butter and jam.

Yesterday we had a family glide up on cross-country skis— mother, father, ten-year-old boy, eight-year-old girl all in good humor, the storm for them a pleasant adventure. And of course we've had people hovering desperately along the edges.

Last night we allowed two hapless guys, Mason and Roger, to spend the night on the restaurant floor. Our preconditions were: no smoking, no noise, and of course, no weapons or drugs. Carlos frisked them, turning his face from their smell.

"No third person can sleep here," Carlos insisted, finger in their faces. "Word gets out that you two have found a sweet spot and the spot disappears. Not to mention the other non-negotiable term—as soon as the temperature goes above freezing, you two return to the street."

They nodded and Carlos barked, drill sergeant style, "Got that, motherfuckers?"

I handed them mops and brushes to wash the floors and scrub the bathrooms—after they'd washed their permanently discolored faces and brushed their grossly decayed teeth with spare toothbrushes I found in the paper-towel closet, back where I'd tried hiding the second-meeting fliers. The guy I think is Mason got a somewhat used, hard bristle toothbrush while the diminutive Roger got a brand new, child's Big Bird number.

Carlos warned them not to wash other parts of their bodies, or even a corner to their clothing. The stench would be too much. Any infraction of the rules, he said, and goodbye Mason, goodbye Roger. "If it comes to that, "*I'll* throw you out. It's my shop." A detail I worry that Carlos forgets: My shop, not his. And I do any throwing necessary.

"Tough Guy," Carlos whispered, his sinewy arm wrapped around me, his lips warming my neck, near my ear, forcing me to focus on the door handle. "If it weren't for me you'd be saddled with those two forever. And don't think they don't know it."

Well, fine, so I probably wouldn't know how to get rid of them. It's as if they're only half here. Mason and Roger stare into space and move with a painstaking, "don't-mind-me" exactness. They're barely visible. Partly a deliberate survival technique, but partly too, I think, the eradicating effect of poverty. Their clothes, their posture, their personalities all are ghostly. You glance at them and glance away. ≈

Enlightenment is Immanent

January 25

Carlos sleeps four hours a night—he starts baking before five —and following his lead, I've found that a half-night of ecstatic REM is infinitely more refreshing than seven straight hours of dumb oblivion. All these years I've been sticking to a single course, a monotonous round: working the shop, closing it late, shoveling in food, skimming a tabloid, falling into bed.

But with Carlos's visit, I've discovered that by doing the same things I've always done, only with more awareness and less sleep, I'm suddenly liberated. The cycle of boredom and disappointment that was my life has become a heart-pounding adventure.

On four hours of sleep, pinpoints of light swim in the air. I am elated to the point of levitating. A phrase fills my mind; my pulse beats with it: *enlightenment is immanent.*

When I asked him today—astounded that I'd never wondered or cared—where he lived, his answer was vague. When I pressed for an address, working hard to suppress my panicky curiosity concerning roommates or other intimates, Carlos said,

"I can't say for certain where my rightful abode is at any one moment. No one can." ≈

Jubilee

Stephanie, whose shift starts at six, rarely arrives before eight. I have to handle the frantic, often vicious commuter crowd solo while Carlos finishes the donuts and moves on to tarts and cakes. When I ask how she justifies this, she says, "No one tips before 8:30. At six and seven, they're fascists."

"How do you know?"

"Trust me, it shows."

Stephanie does what she wants, as she wants, and I have no interest in interfering. Unlike Carlos, she harbors few secrets. She's forty-two years old and lives above a Davis Street beauty salon, where she gives manicures and pedicures, part-time. A long time ago, she was married to a drivers' ed teacher who racked up huge debts on her credit cards. Irritable and competent, with a big square face surrounding pale, bunched up little features, she devotes a good deal of her life to caring for her older sister who has multiple sclerosis. Stephanie's smart and bad tempered, and who can blame her?

With the storm, with Carlos sleeping here, I've been keeping his schedule. I rise instinctively during his meditation and we go downstairs together. He whips up three kinds of dough, then wakes the poor human bundles curled on the front-room floor. I make coffee while Carlos supervises Roger and Mason in the bathrooms. By five we've handed them bagsful of leftovers and sent (more like shoved) them into the cold.

An hour later the aroma of Carlos's baking has overcome any lingering smell of their fitful night on the hard cold floor. The miasma of deprivation, confusion, and illness vanishes with the first batch of donuts, the first hot tray of Danish. The shop reverberates with the grinding of coffee beans, the scalding of cappuccino and hot cocoa.

With the storm, Carlos and I have had only die-hard optimists in the mornings, dressed for business. In the afternoon we've had college kids, the occasional family, and a few giddy young couples, newly, seriously in love. They all seem jubilant, as if the blizzard has granted the world a reprieve from ordinary worries. People who normally push others away are temporarily sympathetic. Because we're all in this together. And there is no other news. ≈

Alone Again

Alone again. I knew it was coming and it did: Carlos is gone. He's gone but he'll return.

Even if seven days is not long enough to establish a routine, let alone what it felt like—a lifelong ritual involving our entire beings—I have absolute faith. Carlos will come back and we'll return forever to the world we so effortlessly made together.

All morning long, I tried to ignore the impending rift. Before, after; then, now. Totally within the moment, I recalled an aphorism about not knowing what you think you know and vice versa. Carlos commented that it was too cold for clouds to form. I answered that that was a myth, cold doesn't affect clouds like that. The sun, though, was blinding; the sky excruciatingly blue; the els and buses running on schedule.

I spent the morning absorbed in details—details were all: the smell of coffee, the wiggly activity of customers, the sound of crockery knocking together, the way my hand looked on the countertop, and oh, a hundred other things at once. My life

was the same now as ever. And whatever happened—
happened. Using all restraint, I tried *not to try*. And yet—there
was no ignoring the crystalline air outside our doors being too
sharp to breathe. Or the rock-solid, six-foot-high snowdrifts
rising from the street.

Paul from Mystic made it through the alley, though. And
Louie's delivery man triple-parked in front and dollied the
flour in through the restaurant. Even old Mr. Downey and old
Mr. Hedlund trudged their way in today, and shook their heads
at the way I do business: letting delivery men in through the
front. Tsk, tsk.

At noon, Carlos whisked off his apron and I knew: *He was
leaving.*

Busy checking the flour order, I fiddled with the paperwork. "There's supposed to be no charge." My voice was
anxious enough to attract Carlos's attention, draw him to me.
He was zipping his jacket, hoisting his backpack. A nasty chill
leapt from my nerves to the pores of my skin.

Had Carlos brought his backpack down at four this morning when we flicked on the lights and beat on pans, rushing out
Mason and Roger? I would have noticed. But I would have
noticed *more* if he'd darted up at some point to fetch it from
the apartment. Yet there it was dangling from his gifted, gloved
fingers. He had his jacket zipped, his stocking hat on his head.

The flour man was saying, "Relax, man," and pointing to
the "ppd." scrawled at the bottom of the page.

If Carlos waved or nodded at me, if he mumbled, "Later,"
I was aware only that as the alley door bounced shut behind

him, the air turned bleak. Everything went flat, everything looked fake. And from then until now, it's been all I can do to force myself to go through the motions—"Hi, good to see you. What can I get you folks?" ≈

Helpless at the Wheel

January 30

I think if I weren't so busy, I would have lost my mind by now. Carlos is still gone; he did not come back last night, or the night before. I can see now how ridiculous it was for me to expect him to. But expect it I did: every time Mason or Roger turned or coughed downstairs, I listened for the next sound, which I was sure would be that of a lock turning, a door opening, Carlos in the kitchen, up the back stairs. Sounds that never came.

I'm doing the work of three, for Stephanie's sister is ill. I make enormous batches of inferior donuts each morning. Pastries—forget it—I've ordered them daily from an extortionist Polish baker on Wabansia. ≈

No Hope

By Saturday afternoon I'd recovered. After all, the man had to go home. Put on fresh clothes, check his mail. And by eight that next evening, serving college kids coffee and brownies to fuel their resumed studies, I was telling myself it was *good* he'd left when he did. After seven straight days and nights, we needed a short spell to take stock of ourselves, clear our heads. Carlos had trusted me to understand the situation tacitly—and I did.

By nine o'clock last night I was absolutely convinced he was on his way here. Friday, Saturday, Sunday, that's long enough. Carlos was going to show up any minute.

To get myself ready, I closed the shop early. A picture was stuck in my mind: myself posed nonchalantly in the narrow arch between entranceway and bedroom as Carlos rushed to explain where he'd been.

Mason and Roger tapped on the front window. Letting them in, I said, "One false move and you guys are on your butts in the snow. No, fuck that: one false *thought*, if you guys still have thoughts." One of them mumbled something at the floor. The one I think of as Mason clutched his crotch.

"All right, all right, I said, furiously, "But hurry." Then I stood outside the men's room, holding the door open and yelling, "Come on, come on, Jeez." I made sweeping motions with my hands. "Wash up and let's go."

Then I kicked the air near where they lay their heads.

Upstairs, I took a long shower. If Carlos should arrive while I was in the middle of luxuriating under the spray, he could just wait on the landing until I was done. Twice while drying myself, I thought I heard him there. Half-naked, I opened the door and peered down the chilly dark—empty—stairwell.

Oh well, better really if his first glimpse of me was while I was busy, fully clothed, hair dried. I put on an ironed white shirt, a sweater vest, and jeans that were tight before the storm.

At ten-thirty I was happily finishing Friday night's wine. He'd arrive in an hour or so, which would be perfect—there'd still be time for him to circle the floor in my robe, iron balls chiming in his dexterous hands.

At midnight I was still telling myself he'd come any minute. At one and two I was listening to every creak, every rustle and sigh. At three I was praying. Preparing myself for four, when he'd arrive for his shift downstairs, turn on the lights and the radio, as if nothing, nothing, *nothing* had ever happened.

I promised myself I'd wait until seven, as I always used to —before the snow.

But at five when he still hadn't come, I raced downstairs and rushed the bums out. No food, no bathroom. I screamed curses, berated their mothers, and locked the front door behind them. Then I turned on the fryer and started a huge batch of cake donuts.

In six years Carlos has never missed work. Now it's five days and counting. At six-thirty I sold eight large cappuccinos to go and a dozen of my inferior donuts. Unlike Carlos's, mine made grease spots on the white paper bags before I'd even finished ringing up the sale.

What if something terrible had happened to him?

At the cash register, I had a cinematic vision of myself behind the wheel of a car. The speedometer was stuck at the far right; the brakes did not exist. And I had to fight the impulse (as a customer had entered) to throw my arms up over my face…

I sold an old man a cup of Lipton's and a plain cake donut and then hurried back to the kitchen, where I found Carlos's unlisted number scrawled in a tiny, ancient address book tucked among the old ledgers. Twice I dialed the number but hung up mid-ring. I made four pans of brownies, because my brownies, if nothing else, are as good as his.

The third time I dialed, a man trying to sound like a woman (or vice versa) said, "This is Venus. How may I help you?"

Then Stephanie burst in, cursing before she'd even gotten her coat off. Where the fuck was Carlos? "Like I'm supposed to serve your lard logs and—hope people tip out of pity?"

Where was Carlos; where was Maggie? "Isn't Maggie," I asked Stephanie, "supposed to waitress with you?"

"That's not what she does. Maggie the waitress; what a laugh." ≈

If Only

Certain hours stand out, shimmering with a surreal glow even as they occur. There's a sudden aura of stillness, a noticeable rise or fall in temperature, and the unmistakable sensation that what is happening to you will turn out to be either so glorious or so wrenching you will end up carrying it with you always.

That whole office Christmas party was like that. Free food, free drink at the ad agency where Colin had worked in the mailroom the summer before. Neither of us had slept all week. Oh maybe we had dozed in each other's arms, but mostly we were too ecstatic, too full of each other, to sustain a state of unconsciousness. If we weren't in class, we were rapt in our room; we were talking nonstop; we were on a marathon trek through the city, alighting finally at the 24-hour Taco Bell for desperately needed food.

By my recollection, our happiness at that party surged to a scary new height. We were drunk before we drank a drop. And then of course, we did drink. We laughed and threw our arms around each other and no one in the whole, overweening advertising agency seemed to notice. A few characters from the mailroom sauntered by and tugged Colin's earring by way of greeting, but otherwise we were alone, toasting one silly thing after another. You know the expression, "walking on air"? At that party, Colin and I hovered near the chandelier, privy to a delicate music emanating from each sparkling prism.

And then—what? We stumbled into the hall, up a set of steps and through a fire door onto the roof. And from that point on, everything was so fast, so fragmentary, that it doesn't fit; it occupies no time. Which may be why, or one reason why, on a primal and primitive level, I've always felt there should be a way to put myself back there. A way to will myself back in time to make what happened not happen, not really, not in the end. ≈

Be a Man and Ask

February 3

A dismal omen: the first customer this morning was an old woman with shoe polish in her hair, who handed me a dollar bill (sixty-two cents short but I couldn't bear to quibble) that was translucent from age, as soft and warm as living tissue.

Then after a slow, dreary day, at 8:00 p.m., with the shop empty—relief and fury. He appeared! Breezed in with the voluptuous, beautiful Maggie Townsend, on his arm. I watched from behind the swinging door as she slid out of her ankle-length coat, wiggled in her low-cut dress, and squirmed in her chair. And from where I stood, Carlos the militant ascetic, Carlos the nonpracticing homosexual, seemed oddly flushed. His attention horribly, peculiarly riveted.

Stephanie's block-shaped backside obscured my view. As if she knew. Or not *as if*—of course she knew! Maroon hair bristling, she asked if they wanted my "artery cloggers?"

Then as Carlos's covert operative, she stepped far enough left for me to see him ease himself free from his leather jacket and smooth an Irish sweater over his chest. He was telling

Maggie that he couldn't recommend anything except maybe my brownies. I watched him take off his fleece stocking cap. His hair was loose, clean for a change, and to tell the truth, beautiful. He reached for the girl's pale, plump hand and pressed it to his 47-year-old mouth.

I clutched the doorway.

Maggie leaned over the table, her big tits pressing into it as she whispered passionately. A second later, the vicious Stephanie caught me watching them, and with a snide grin, flapped their receipt. "Pellegrinos, Malcolm. No ice. No brownies."

I had six carrot cakes baking. Vaguely aware I was hyperventilating, I began crossing the room to take them out of the oven, when I felt his breath on the back of my neck. He touched my shoulder, traced a line down my spine to my waist. If I hadn't bitten my tongue I'd have moaned out loud. As it was, my traitorous body shuddered with unmistakable, horrible, pleasure.

"You can always tell a true saint," he whispered, "by how long and how hard he resists." I wheeled around, confused and desperate. Because the words were his, the breath, the touch—but the voice was Stephanie's! And it was she who was standing there, grabbing my belt loops.

She narrowed her mean little eyes, released me abruptly, and said, "Go on. March on out there, Malcolm. Be a man, and just—ask." ≈

Flattery Will Get You Everywhere

February 4

Well, they did it. They convinced me to give it another try. Carlos and Stephanie and Maggie Townsend spent half the night coercing me into giving the meetings another chance. We're planning one more—and should it fail, *last*—meeting in two weeks.

Why, I asked again, if they thought the idea was so "crucial" as Carlos kept saying, did I need to be involved? Why didn't they start a theology group without me?

Because," Maggie said, "to succeed, the group needs a holy leader."

"Why?" I asked.

"Because otherwise it'll devolve into a coffee klatch with pretensions."

"So you be the one."

Tossing her head, Maggie mock-checked everyone's face to see if she dared to speak. "Hard to believe in this day and age," she said, "but it's still more difficult for women."

"A problem," Stephanie feigned astonishment, "with divinely inspired female leadership? You've got to be kidding."

"Okay, okay." I waved that issue away. "Then why not you, Carlos? You're always saying you know how these things work."

"Exactly. And they don't work with someone like me at the top. Whereas *you*, Malcolm, if you'd only apply yourself— could qualify as a bona fide saint."

"Oh yeah? Just how vain, and how stupid, do you think I am?"

"I've watched you for very closely, Malcolm; I know what I'm talking about. You're a true innocent. You're wildly non-materialistic and you go into these spells of communing with the universe, where you're really, I mean really, out there."

"Oh yeah?" Despite myself, I leaned back, grotesquely flattered. ≈

Religion Without Rules

February 5

Sometimes the more you swear something's dead and gone—over and done with—the more inevitable that it pops up to prove you wrong.

Carlos had taken it upon himself to close the shop. He'd opened the front door and yelled at Mason and Roger. "Hey, you guys, the shelters miss you." He'd cupped a hand to his ear. "Hear that? They're calling your names."

Two minutes later a rock cracked the plate-glass window. Carlos stopped rolling my hand around in one of those elaborate, comical-if-they-weren't-so-infuriating handshakes and pulled a spool of duct tape from deep in his pocket. Without missing a beat, he taped the broken window while Maggie Townsend, chin on hands, eyes over-bright, asked me pertinent, half-adoring questions about the "enlightened discussion group." She tossed her blonde curls and said she could feel it in the air: Something fantastic was about to happen.

Carlos was back to caressing the inside of my forearm. It

took everything I had, life-or-death restraint, to hold myself immobile.

"Don't you hear it all the time?" Maggie asked. "That hum rising to a buzz?" She personally was ready to dedicate herself to freeing legions of thwarted souls.

"What?" Upset about the window and determined to ignore Carlos, whose excruciating touch kept burning my arm, I asked Maggie how she and Carlos knew each other. What was their connection?

Lavishing even more attention on me, Maggie said, "From tai chi." They had taken a class together at the Y and had considered each other "best friends" ever since.

Best friends? I couldn't tell whether this was a romantic euphemism or a simple, plain truth. But nothing's simple. Maggie Townsend talked too much. She wiggled in her seat and ran nervous fingers through her bleached hair. Her avidness was embarrassing in a way that made me like her. And, by now I was positive: No matter what she and Carlos shared ideologically, sexually they were impossible. Carlos was the archetypal secular gay monk. While poor, needy Maggie Townsend was obviously, tortuously "straight."

I liked her, too, because she agreed with me about the first meeting. "False euphoria can be dangerous," she told Carlos. "It was insulting how you set Malcolm up."

(My problem is I don't get out enough. If someone agrees with me on something more significant than decaffeinated vanilla-scented French roast, I am beside myself. Someone agrees with me on worship and it's as if she's saved my life.)

Fresh coffee and big squares of my carrot cake appeared before us. Stephanie served so unobtrusively, you'd think she had invisible powers. Pooling over, down and around each perfect square of cake was a luscious pineapple-cream cheese sauce that only Carlos could have concocted.

"Okay," he said. "So maybe the last meeting didn't reach total rapture. Still, it was—it *was* perfect." Carlos was running his knuckles lightly, swiftly along my leg, "If you got carried away, Malcolm, it's because the meeting took on a life of its own. And isn't that the way it's supposed to be? No one person running it, no one dictating how things should go?"

(Did I tell him that? It was my guiding principle, but did I ever say so out loud? No. Not to anyone.) "I never planned this far."

"No rules," Carlos said, "and ritual will develop spontaneously."

"Where are you getting this, Carlos?"

Stephanie, who was serving me more coffee and cake, said, "It's not so hard to figure out. Religion without rules. Everybody has their say."

"Who's talking about *religion?*" I yelled.

"No one," Carlos said. "No one is talking about it explicitly. But..."

"But what? You think you can read my mind?"

"Our theology group," Carlos said, "may not have anything to do with religion, *per se*, but it is life-affirming, a forum for the whys and wherefores of life and death."

"Really! And, how the fuck do you know?"

"Because, Malcolm, I know whereof I speak."

He was caressing my shoulder, one satiny brown hand squeezing the back of my neck. I dragged my finger through the leftover sauce, and was raising it to my mouth, when he swooped in and sucked it off. Sly with mischief, Carlos swirled his fingertips over my plate, and then over his. He wagged five silken pineapple-cream cheese caps in front of my face. "No thanks." I averted my eyes. He smacked his lips. "Oo-yum!" But when I looked again, his sauce-covered fingers were still there in front of my face, waiting to be licked. ≈

Carlos the Manipulator

Ninety-nine percent of the time I'm sure they're right: You don't give up after one try. But when I close my eyes there's a nameless but familiar face there, winking and grinning at how stupid I am. Carlos is back at work—and thank God (no questions asked, no answers given), sleeping on my couch at night.

Tonight when I said his plan for reviving the meetings carried whiffs of conspiracy, he wrapped his arms around me from behind. I was standing at the counter, opening another bottle of Côtes du Rhone. Carlos had been taking his bath; it was easier for me to mention "conspiracy" when he was in another room. But suddenly, there he was, close behind me, wrapped in a towel. The ends of his hair were wet and warm beads of water were sliding down his arms, on to my arms. His almost regrown mustache brushed my face. "That mentality, Malcolm, is what makes you so perfect."

I did not even try not to tremble. Carlos is old and there are places where his skin is wrinkled but he's lean and brown, and thick greenish veins swell over his sinewy muscles so that you can see (and for the first time I can *feel*) them pulse. For a second I thought he was going to throw me to the floor—and then he was at the other end of the room, clothed in my robe.

Crossing his brave-looking, high-arched feet, he leaned against the doorjamb and said, "That lunatic fringe mind-frame is what makes you so perfect as a spiritual leader."

After managing a long, steadying sip of wine, I asked, "How so?"

"Because it shows such extraordinary ability to look past everyday logic." He shook his head and laughed. "Conspiracy nuts are the ultimate believers. Think about it, Malcolm. What is faith but the ability to see connections that are not completely there?" ≈

Nothing, Nothingness, and No More

February 8

That was two days ago, and what happened this morning was nothing. I know that. *It was nothing!* My only excuse for even thinking about it is that it's late. I can't sleep. And I can hear Carlos sleeping in the next room.

At five this morning, before Maggie and Stephanie's arrival, Carlos was cracking eggs into the vat. I was leaning against the wall, still half-dreaming, so this next non-occurrence might only have been a figment.

My eyes were half-closed and Carlos came over and placed his hands along either side of my face. He stepped closer, pressing his body into mine. And then, cradling the back of my head, he kissed me, running his tongue over the front of my teeth at first and then pushing the tip along the roof of my mouth. Then, with a little push, he said, "Leave everything to me." ≈

Hunger

Before he went to bed tonight, while I worked on my diary, Carlos snuck up behind me and placed his lips and tongue against the nape of my neck. I jumped in alarm and my hand flew up, covering the computer screen. Laughing, he put set his twin sets of iron balls in their little nests inside their little embroidered boxes. Poking me under my chin, he said, "Hey, what do you think? I don't respect your privacy?"

I did not look up. Being around him all the time has become really exhausting. Especially because, since he's come back, I don't know why, but I cannot sleep.

"Start thinking of your Life and Times, in terms of a 'Doctrine.' "

"What?"

"And remember, Malcolm, choose your demons carefully."

"Doctrine? Demons? Since when?"

"Your big sin, silly. The thing you and your followers can never get away from. Will it be sex? *Food?*" And he patted the cushion of fat that's been forming over my belt. Ever since Carlos's return I've been nervously, guiltily stuffing my face. ≈

Sleepless

I really cannot sleep at all. Tonight after midnight, Carlos brought out a great platter of meat loaf and freshly mashed potatoes, a bowl of creamed spinach, and a basket of warm rolls, and butter. He handed me a frosted stein of Heinekens. And set on the table a deep-dish apple pie with a huge, heavy wedge of extra sharp Cheddar. Then he tottered off to the couch where he instantly sank into deep and enviable sleep. ≈

Carlos the Virtuoso

All this week and last, the fillings were cherry or strawberry or raspberry. Almost everything's heart-shaped, even the bread. And, I've done all the things I always do the first half of February—dug out the Valentine paraphernalia, tacked up sprays of ribbon and lace and cardboard cupids. But somehow I failed to connect the concept with the day. As if not me but some zombie were setting out the paper hearts.

Weird what fear will do. I think it's fear: In my heart of hearts I always thought if I got to this point, my personal answer for why I was born would appear in front of me, or rise up from my inner being. If nothing else, I would recognize it as handwriting on the wall.

I remember making up fliers with Maggie, quibbling over the layout, the typeface, all conceivable nuances—*except the date.* **"New Forms"** was what we decided on. Open, vague. **"Everybody Welcome!"** And even our quibbling appears in my mind as a brief, jumpy scene of my arms flailing, Maggie elaborately sighing.

This morning, it finally hit me—February 14! How stupid could I be? Carlos had the music on. He had the iron balls going. I was struggling to button my jeans. Only a couple of weeks ago, remember, I'd happily slipped into a pair that had been too tight for years. But since then, I haven't stopped eating. And Carlos, who's always thrown a fit if I even *looked* like I wanted to taste anything, has been foisting food on me: tarts, cakes, pastries stuffed with fabulously sick, rich fillings, and double fudge brownies topped with whipped cream. At night, sumptuous native cooking: guacamoles and fresh beef tacos, spicy burritos and enchiladas smothered in silken white cheese.

So, I sucked in hard, once, twice, and then, my sorry effort with the metal button a constrained success, I broke into a revelatory sweat. I huffed and puffed, and my scalp tingled as I realized the next meeting was scheduled for *Valentine's* Day!

"Let me get this straight," Carlos said. "You think people who come to the meetings are going to say, 'Holy crap! I can't go out tonight; it's Valentine's Day'?"

"And you think it won't affect business if we've got a bunch of misfits sitting around talking about whether a personal relationship with God is possible?"

Carlos tossed his waist-length hair behind him. He circled the room on the balls of his feet. And as usual, the sight of his powerful calves and ankles in motion made me pant. The evil, alluring Carlos, a beatific grin on his face, set his twin sets of iron balls in their nests. Still grinning, he swayed on those wondrous feet as the raggedy terry cloth robe my mother gave me ten Christmases ago began to slip off his skinny Mexican shoulders, the frayed tie having come loose from his twenty-six inch waist.

Circling silently behind me, he rose on his toes (Carlos is short: five-five, five-six at most) and pressed his hands on my shoulders. Then I felt his brindled hair on my cheek, grazing my ear and then (God Help Me) the pouch of new flesh at my neck.

Jostling me, he said, "Come on, Malcolm. Forget the stupid store."

His hands moved along my back and I bit the inside of my cheek.

"Forget the fucking store!" Carlos dug at the area where my legs join my trunk.

"We are about to embark," he said, "on a totally new, life-everlasting kind of venture. All that matters from now on, Malcolm, are endeavors of the *soul.*"

"Yes." I held my breath. The robe shifted and swayed behind me with Carlo's small sinewy body. He ran his hands up and down the length of my arms, the flaps of that robe opening away from him.

"The time," he whispered, "is *perfect,*" and pressed his hand on my painfully constrained penis, which angled huge and hard along my thigh.

"The time, the time, the time," Carlos said, "is now!"

His fingertips tapped on the tip and in my extremity, I put myself out of the world. Whatever happened next, I told myself, happened. There was nothing I could do. No move I could make, no sound, no silent wish would change what

Carlos had in mind. Quivering and panting, I tried to pretend that what we were enacting was nothing more than an intricate kind of handshake. While Carlos kept stroking, kept pressing, kept rubbing, I gathered all my consciousness to keep from moaning.

At this point, at this crucial—I beg you, Carlos, please just one more second—he managed to make it both better and worse by moving his hands up and away, his fingers near my chest before mercifully he drew me closer to him. He hugged me from behind. With the robe open, I recognized his tight muscled torso rubbing against me, his hip points jabbing my butt cheeks, squashed down and together by my way too-small jeans.

But I was not, was not, was *not* going to groan and gasp, shiver and come. I refused to think of his nakedness. I suppressed a fantasy involving the terry cloth belt knotted around his wrists, tied up over his head, so he dangled from the ceiling. And I stalwartly resisted the image of myself yanking out his long brown hair, strand by strand, so as to hear *him* groan.

Instead, I imagined freezing to death on a tundra in Alaska. Lost among a sea of glaciers, I considered an arctic wall of cryogenically frozen heads. Hundreds and hundreds of them stored among the ice floes. Superfrozen heads submerged in one endless million-year-old glacier.

No good, of course. Carlos's fingers were gliding along my bigger-fatter-softer-every-day belly. He caressed my padded chest and pressed hard against my backside. He was saying,

"You're ready for this, Malcolm." And then the act of a virtuoso—his hands swept down and away. "Come on, come on," he hissed, and my lungs flew open, my eyes rolled in their sockets.

"Oh God, Carlos." I screamed and hopped and then I really gave it up: choking, crying, thrashing. Carlos laughed and reached for me, saying, "Hey easy, baby, easy. Are you all right?"

Soon I was in the bathroom, struggling again with the impossibly taut fabric and the metal button, trying now to rip my dampened clothes off. But everything was slippery and it took a while. Eventually I worked it out, forcing the openings apart. I wormed up and out and peeled down the pants, yanking the shrunken T-shirt over my head. From the hamper I pulled out a sweat shirt and pants, which (thank you God), stretched out effortlessly, as much as necessary. When I emerged, Carlos had his hair braided. Dressed in crisp, checked slacks and a pristine white shirt open at his ropey throat, he was already at the stove, making breakfast.

"I'm not hungry," I said.

He kept cooking and whistling and after a while, piled a plate with tortillas, chorizo, fried eggs, hash browns and beans. He put the plate in front of me, between flatware and a cloth napkin. He turned and brought a bottle of my favorite green hot sauce to the table.

"I'm not hungry," I said.

He poured two big glasses of orange juice and sat down. He drank his juice but I did not touch mine. He tasted a bit of the chorizo. I tapped my fork. He took another taste and I looked away. The struggle with him, with myself in the bathroom—had left me weak. He gulped juice, chewed sausage, and stared at me. I crossed my arms, lifted my chin and stared back. He dabbed his mouth and rolled a tortilla. As he chewed, I gave in and sipped the fresh orange juice. I drummed my fingers. As Carlos rolled a fragrant floury tortilla around a fried egg and refried beans, doused in green chili sauce, I nibbled at one small fiery bit of the sausage. Without looking at him, I put my fork down. I stood up and walked to the threshold, stopped and sighed. Okay. Carlos wins. I sat back down and ate a spoonful of hot, spicy beans. He was bringing me coffee with cinnamon, heavy with condensed milk, plus extra sugar. I've started every day with coffee since I was twelve. So, thanking him, I slurped it down, waited, and slurped down the rest. As he refilled my cup, I closed my eyes, waiting perhaps as long as a minute. But then I sighed and shrugged, venturing another tiny taste of sausage. At some point, I covered my face with my hands. And then somewhere in here I rocked in my chair. But before I knew it, I'd scarfed down that whole vast Mexican breakfast.

Carlos patted my cheeks, which I could tell were red. He said, "You, Malcolm Tully, are going to be truly great at this."

As we turned off the lights and I lumbered ahead of him, grunting down the squeaky stairs, he bent to ruffle the hair on top of my head. "People want this, lover. They want it, need it, and you're the only one who can give it to them." ≈

Losing It

In my vision of an enlightened discussion group when I imagined "my turn to speak my mind," the speaking aspect was metaphorical. The challenge was just to get to where everyone had found a seat, cleared his throat and blown his nose. When it really was finally time for me to say what's what, a higher order would kick in.

What do I *think?* Why am I *alive?* Bottom line: I need to believe in something greater than myself, which, come on; can't be *that* hard to find! ≈

Stupefied

It's after midnight, but Stephanie has joined Maggie and Carlos in the apartment. So I guess they're anxious, too. Maggie's calling, "Come out, Malcolm. Come out, come out, wherever you are." But I'm drowsy and naked, and wish they would go away.

With my door closed, the covers over my head, I'm still aware of Carlos coolly reviewing the plans. Maggie murmurs agreeably and Stephanie mutters. Stephanie, I found out, visits her sister, the one with MS, in a nursing home every night after her shift. She's worked with me for six years and until a few weeks ago, I knew only that she has a relentlessly sour disposition and wears—every time I've ever seen her—a cheap black skirt, white nylon blouse, white stockings, and off-brand athletic shoes.

Maggie's perpetual motion—I can hear her boots on the floor—seems at this remove like a peculiar, feminine form of anger.

Why doesn't Carlos shoo the females away? They linger

and fuss and he says nothing, even though it's late. They fume and sputter and I have to pee but do not want to see or be seen. If they weren't here, John Coltrane's saxophone would fill the apartment.

If Maggie and Stephanie weren't here, Carlos would be curled beside me, feeding me. He'd be getting ready to take his bath. The windows would have misted up and he'd start circling the rooms. The robe would slip from his thin brown frame and the glint from the iron balls in his hands would break through the blanket dimness. If the women weren't here, I'd be swirling Metaxa in a glass, watching him. Drunk but still drinking, stuffed but still eating, I'd suck in every detail: Carlos's tantalizing, unspoken bribes hanging in the air; me stupefied with the awful hope that he might pull me from the chair, might hold me, might sway with me while the horns sounded and the bells chimed. ≈

Before the Meeting

February 14

Miraculously, I managed to slip out well before dawn, before Carlos woke. I left a printout for him:

> *Hope you don't mind, Carlos, but I'm taking the day off. Don't worry; I'll be back for the meeting. And I'm leaving you the station wagon. Have you noticed how the raspberry twists have been selling? Since it's Valentine's Day, would you consider doubling the batches? Please also make fruit and custard tarts, those giant macaroons, éclairs, tortes and Black Forest cake. Thanks. M.*

I bundled myself into a moss-colored anorak, this year's Christmas gift from my parents. Trimmed with coyote fur, it is supposed to keep you warm to fifty below. My scarf and gloves lay on the coffee table near the sofa where Carlos was sleeping. Standing there, I could feel a sheet of cold air from the window above his head. Yet he lay oblivious on the undersized sofa—only half the army blanket covering him. Light from a streetlamp emphasized the furrows in his face. His hair flowed over the armrest. His inside arm was pressed into the sofa back and his outside arm was flung over his head, the underside of his biceps looking as sleek and lively as a quick brown fish.

The sight of Carlos dreaming, unawares, unprotected and half-naked set me trembling. His offhand pats and extra-casual gropes, his ardent new habit of plying me with narcotically rich food and the flurry of inconsequential kisses with which he rewards me for consuming staggering amounts of it—are more intimate than anything that's happened to me since Colin died. As I hovered over him, Carlos shifted in his sleep. His arm dropped to the floor. He turned on his side and the scratchy wool blanket slid lower along his flank. Stepping backwards, I inhaled hard at the sight of his gleaming hipbone. He was snoring and I watched his top leg kick free. For the hundredth time I took in the breath-taking curve of his instep. With his feet, his hugely perfect ankles, and the swell of those calves, you'd think he could jump a mile in the sky.

Determined not to wake him, I still hovered, swearing that any second now, just one more second, and I'd hurry away. Go, I told myself. Go on! Go *now!*

If the next meeting was going to happen, I had to have the day off, away from everything. But if Carlos were to raise an eyelid by so much as a millimeter—I'd be snared inside his net of crisscrossing seductions.

Asleep, he looked both old and not-so-old. His features looked softer, his body even more impossibly lithe. The little wrinkles on his sharp thin face did not exist, but the delicate red capillaries looping over his nose, across his cheeks suggested a map of ancient configurations. His hard-to-keep-brown mustache brought to mind father-animal traits, like the tufts of the oldest, wisest owl. But beneath this gleamed a lush red mouth, the satiny lower lip just slightly agape and (enough to kill me), vividly tender.

Gasping for air, I gripped my jacket, ready to tear it off. My heart pounded wildly and in my frenzy I somehow—unbelievably—got away.

On the street, stunned by the cold black expanse, by the shockingly limitless space, I hurried into the pharmacy doorway. A dire anxiety rose up and within seconds I was hyperventilating through a flood of tears. It was three-thirty in the morning. I didn't stop weeping for a full, eternal five minutes. And then, frightened and humiliated, I staggered over the glittering pavement, wondering what had just happened.

No one witnessed it. But surely I was not the only one sobbing then; not the only one quaking in sorrow. Isn't the question: Why *shouldn't* we cry? Isn't it an outright miracle that we aren't all weeping all the time? Because being alive right now is just way too much—and not enough. Amazingly, we nonetheless march through our paces, day after day, year after year. "Hi, how are you?" "Good, thanks. And you?"

And no one protests, no one rebels!

Or maybe they do. Maybe I've got it all wrong. Maybe crying in the street is a universal secret. While I'm off tallying inventories, working the cash register, padding haplessly about my apartment, everyone else is outside screaming with abandon, expressing sorrow, disappointment as well as blessed giddy joy—everything, everything all the time!

And then—I admit: probably not. Prolonged laughter or crying of the kind I just went through skirts the edge of transcendence. It gives us intimations of life beyond our grasp. My little attack has left me more fragile than cleansed. But the swing and strangeness of it suggest a passageway. What if I did teeter there, all but directly within God's Presence? Absent the usual warped politics; absent especially that master-slave routine?

Trudging south, into a stinging wind on Sheridan Road, I hopped on the first bus coming my way. In the dark sky no stars shined, no trace of color encroached. The lighting inside the bus rendered the riders woeful and unwholesome. The man across from me wore a Burberry scarf and a Burberry coat. He balanced a briefcase on his lap and was reading what looked like a legal brief. He kept tugging at his collar. In a seat facing the front, a round faced, middle aged woman appeared asleep, her head back, resting against the molded beige plastic. A few seats behind her, a teenage boy and girl, their faces painted like Kabuki masks, rocked to and fro, arms and legs entwined.

There were a few nurse-type women, their pastel uniforms showing beneath their big down coats. And one more: Craning my neck, I noticed a hairy man encased in reflective running gear. He wore an orange cap and his shiny silver gloves fingered a waist-length beard divided into two stiff conical shapes.

The notion came to me that people who ride the four a.m.

bus are desperately clinging to whatever's slipping away from them. Awake at this hour, they experience a separateness some of us have never imagined. I glanced at their expressions: the weariness, the determination, pain and loss. Everyone around me needed that chance to stand up and say what's most important. This bus was full of seekers.

I don't have any fliers to hand out, but I had such a strong feeling, I decided, why not at least check? Eyes burning (the air raw with diesel fumes), I rummaged in my backpack and, yes! Found the manila envelope stuffed with fliers. I hadn't put it there, but there it was.

So I stomped up the aisle, shoving copies of the "New Forms" printout in people's faces, explaining, of course, that the topic isn't set in stone and, really, anyone can talk about anything. My voice was hoarse, maybe from crying so hard before, maybe because what I was doing was so unlike me.

Then the bus lurched and stopped, and the driver was out of his seat, yelling, "Hey, you! No soliciting on my bus!" Right behind me was a bearish man in several Alaskan-type sweaters, whom I hadn't noticed before. "Say, my good man," he said in the overarticulated pseudo-cosmopolitan accent sometimes affected by winos. "I'd be interested in one of your religious pamphlets."

"No, that's all right. They're nothing, really."

"Oh, but obviously they are something." Setting down what looked like a bowling bag he dug into one sweater's pocket and offered me whiskey from a brown bag. The bus driver was making his way up the aisle, coming at us.

"No, thank you," I said, handing him a flier and hurrying away.

I got back late in the afternoon. "Already five p.m.," Carlos said and he told Maggie and Stephanie to mind the shop. We were going upstairs. "Don't disturb us," he said.

They scoffed. "Don't worry."

Inside the apartment Carlos already had candles burning. The waning winter light faded behind sheer curtains I didn't recall hanging there. We drank Grande Dame Clicquot. There was a wheel of runny cheese, which I scooped up with toasted rusks. Undoing his hair, Carlos sat close to me on the sofa. He crossed his legs and draped an arm around me. "You know what's going on, with us and the meetings, but more between *us*, is fantastic. As if heaven sent." Patting my knee, he rose and slipped into the kitchen.

The champagne bottle was wrapped in a towel and clumsy me spilt some. Carlos appeared, put a tray of chocolate strawberries on the table, and knelt down to mop up the effervescent little puddle. I watched the tips of his hair get wet. It's a mind-control technique, I know: starve a person before unexpectedly offering a solitary feast. But that doesn't explain my totally out-of-control desire.

Irresistibly sinister and strong, Carlos cuddled beside me. "Strawberries," he said, plucking one from the platter and holding it to my mouth. Pressing his fingers against my lips, he fed me one coated berry after another.

We drank more champagne. And after a lull, when he resumed pressing the chocolate strawberries into my mouth, I grabbed twin handfuls of his hair, winding it tight around my wrists as if *that* could restrain me. I shifted my buttocks, trying to redistribute my weight, when Carlos slid on top of me, his small skinny chest resting against my fat shirtless self. His long arms reaching for the plate, he continued pushing the strawberries between my lips, followed now by the tip of his tongue. (But every time I tried to bite that tip, it darted out.)

The sound system moved to Gregorian chants, which Carlos did not expect. He got up and I sat up, edging myself forward to guzzle more champagne.

"Are you all right?" Carlos asked. "Your face is red."

I stood and looked at myself in the mirror. Hands under my pecs, I said, "Carlos, look! I'm growing breasts."

He said, "That does it," leading me to bed, where I performed mightily. At first, he tried telling me how to go about it. But fat, drunk—even after years of nothing—I'm still a master at the ever-varying gradations between pleasure and pain. I still know how to make a man scream. ≈

Flight

I've discovered I can fly! I am flying now. After a lifetime of fear, it turns out that none of my inadequacies matter. I soar over and under the backs of clouds.

The meeting convened. The shop was packed. I wavered, cold and numb, on a ledge. The crowd below blurred to a pattern of colors; their voices rose, and fell silent. I took a breath, my mind shut down—and I jumped. But instead of plummeting, I floated. My hands fluttered and words spun from my mouth in fanciful loops.

I'm not sure how long I spoke or what I said. But it seemed natural, or no, *supernatural.* As if the reason I was born really *was* to say what I said!

Who would have guessed?

Well, Carlos.

Carlos guessed against the odds. I mean, what could be more unlikely? Coax me from the boat and I'll walk on water. Toss me off a cliff and I'll sprout wings. Shove me in front of the microphone and I'll sway the masses. It was only a guess, though. When I finished speaking, Carlos was astonished, overjoyed, waiting behind the swinging doors. He slapped my cheeks and pounded my back. We leaped together, trying not to shout or laugh, tears streaming down both our faces. Then Maggie slipped in with us, and when Stephanie joined, we danced in a circle. Embracing in the kitchen, the four of us mouthed the words: *"We did it, we did it, we did it!"*

But *I* especially did it! I went out there and talked for two straight hours about how unsavory the old master-slave forms of worship seem in modern context. About the dangers inherent in spiritual ambition, which set us running on roads that no longer connect to anything. How we are taught routines that thousands of years ago may have evoked an experience of God, but which—since we have done nothing *new* with them, nothing to make them our own—no longer apply.

"If you currently practice a formal religion," I said, "chances are, no matter how fervent your feelings, you end up just going through the motions. Be honest. Who's familiar with genuine spiritual uplift?"

No one answered. "Okay, no one. Though some of you," I shouted, "may think you do. A shiver, a moment of déjà vu; a trembling desire that out of the darkness of your soul a flowering of hope might bloom?

"Isn't that—" I claimed as undeniable, "as close as we ever come? The stray tear for no reason? The frisson of joy or fear that cuts through the static?

"These are indicators," I said. "But nothing more. Shadows of shadows.

"And those of you who've renounced the *cheesiness* of modern life? Who are leery of manufactured sentiment? Sick unto death of cartoon evangelists, commercials and news segments, this week's recorded idiocy? You know who you are. Are you *here*?

"Are you?"

Silence.

But nothing fazed me. Nothing.

More silence.

I raised a palm, stopped, and whistled softly, opening my eyes wide, casting pale lightning throughout the room.

"This is not a rhetorical question," I said. "I'm asking you about *wonderment*. Some of us are prone to visitations, even though we're all-too-familiar, as subjects and witnesses, to pain and suffering. Be brave," I said, lovely ripples running over my body, the swell of my flesh buoying me along, "We're bereft of faith because the forms are old. They no longer refer to us.

"And yet," I said, "there *is* a world apart from this. We still believe in Omniscience and Omnipotence. We still even worship It. Or we would if we could figure out how to do so without groveling.

"That's something we do to our bosses, for money, for job security. But treating God with the same smarmy self-abasement we use with the district manager is gross, don't you think? We need *new forms* if we're going to talk about God; if we're going to give glory to God."

Spreading my arms, I said, "How lost we are. We need to

pray that purity will come to us. An untarnishable song, a perfect logic."

Scanning the patchwork of colors, I dallied among the subtle but intoxicating ether. Buoyed by the wonderful expanse of my body under the great fluid white gown Carlos had talked me into wearing, my head back, hair streaming, I said that in much older cultures than ours, people take solace in visits from the apparitions of their ancestors. But when they begin to adopt Western culture, they no longer receive such visits, experiencing instead headaches and back aches, ulcers and colitis. Voices, visions, unaccountable aches and pains are manifestations of the same thing. What the manifestations mean—spectral ancestors or migraine headaches—is impossible to fathom. But haven't we all experienced momentary dislocations, flickering existential confusions of *life everlasting*. Haven't we?" I thundered. "Haven't we *all?*"

Evidently we had: The room erupted; the crowd cheered, their hands clapping, feet stamping as I surged here and there. "What we need," I said, "what the doctors, the patients, all of us need are *new forms!*"

I alighted back on the platform, the rippling white gown settling against my damp skin. Applause rang out and I closed my eyes against pinpoints of sweat. With everyone still cheering, I dove through the swinging doors, straight into Carlos's arms. ≈

Success Won't Change Me

A hundred times a day I pat my pockets for credentials that don't exist. The ground beneath me rushes up. The audience: Wait a minute! Can you believe I'm now calling them the *audience*? The whole point was that each person—not just me but *each person*—was supposed to go to the mike and say what it is that matters most. Remember? That was the primary goal!

But two minutes into my spiel, the attendees became *followers*. And in less than no time, I succumbed to their applause. I looked out on what seemed like an ocean of people swaying to the sound of my voice and waving their arms. In my mind, lavender-colored fog swirled at my feet; a profusion of lighters illuminated the darkness. And miracle never ending, tomorrow night I'm scheduled to give—and to get—more of the same!

Which is not to say I've forgotten the original idea. It's just that, if I believe Stephanie, a hundred-some people were so spellbound that with no prompting, they tucked tens and twenties into her hands as she squeezed through the haphazard aisles of chairs. Whether they saw this as the unasked-for price of admission or as a contribution to the cause, I still don't know.

After the crowd filed out in an excited hush, Maggie and Stephanie and Carlos and I stood still for a while in the suddenly quiet, suddenly empty shop. Maggie swept the floor. Stephanie aligned the tables. Carlos locked the doors. I shut off the lights. We drifted upstairs, drank wine and listened to Tibetan bowl music.

Stephanie, as usual, couldn't stand to ignore the obvious. She wriggled big wads of bills out of her apron pockets. "Here," she said, "let's talk about this." Swearing to stick a needle in her eye, she said "my followers" had taken it upon themselves to press money on her.

"We need to put the money into a special account," Carlos said. "I know you don't want to call it a religion, Malcolm. But it needs to be non-taxable. For the I.R.S. And it needs a name. For the bank."

"What do you have in mind, Carlos?"

"It's your call, Malcolm. You're the prophet."

"I'm supposed to pull a name out of a hat?"

"Nothing elaborate. But come up with something now."

"Like what? Jehovah's Heretics? Malcolm's Meek Seekers?"

"Make it believable. Nothing cute."

"What do you think of," Maggie asked, " *Religion Without Rules*'?"

Carlos said, "That's good. RWR. That should do."

Why not? Religion Without Rules sort of disavows real

religion. No rules, no hierarchy, even if I'm the mouthpiece. That was that—no worries.

Still, Carlos satisfied looked even more nefarious than Carlos plotting. Between Stephanie, Maggie, and Carlos, there were four bundles of money, four canvas pouches. And despite my exultation, I couldn't look at Carlos without suspecting him of arranging special folds of fabric inside his vest. Any second I expected the scene in front of my eyes to change into a million little birds fluttering off in a million directions at once.

But I saw it with my own eyes. The meeting took in almost *twenty-two hundred dollars*! Two thousand, one hundred, eighty-six dollars, and seventy-five cents. $2,186.75. The number thrills me, though I know it shouldn't.

Or if it does, I should, quick, give the money all back. Except it's not mine. It belongs to Religion Without Rules. Which is off the ground now; way up and running. And *that's* what's thrilling, not the money, not the amount, but what it proves: that we are undeniably on the right track. Anytime people throw money at you, you must be doing something right.

Even before Carlos counted it, he was so excited he grabbed my face and kissed my mouth. Maggie and Stephanie squealed, digging it out of their uniforms.

"I *knew* it," Carlos said, jumping up and down. "Time is with us on this thing. Whatever we want to happen is happening as we speak!"

(Well, really, as *I* speak, but of course I didn't mention this. Carlos who basically preempted my program—the concept was mine, all he did was adjust the mike—comes on like he's God the Father and I'm the Son. I mean, I do the talking, I deliver the sermons—and in the end I'm the one who's going to get nailed.)

Oh, all right, sorry. Forgive me, One True Almighty One. It's in no way Your Sublime Fault that Carlos has quit juggling the iron balls. Quit even looking at me; I mean *at all!* He's quit playing music—not one recording of rain falling or surf pounding, no chants, no Tibetan bowls, no saxophones, nothing.

"There is not time for that now." That's what he said Friday night. *There is no time for that*, and he zapped off Charles Mingus. Ever since I fucked him, Carlos gives off a palpable air of: Do not disturb. He's fed me nothing, and not touched me once!

That is, until after tonight's meeting, when Maggie and Stephanie heaped money on the table. There was so much! So much that Carlos got carried away and gave me this big gift: He spontaneously grabbed my face and kissed my mouth.

Like I should be: *Thank you, Carlos! Oh! Thank you, thank you!* ≈

Let the Games Begin

Baptism by Humiliation. Enlightenment through Remorse.

A honey-soaked voice-over follows me around, testifying to all that I endure.

The Prophet Rises Before Dawn, Cleanses and Girds Himself. In Perpetual Hunger, He Imbibes a Scalding Elixir, Waits on Customers, Calls on Suppliers.

To get through the day I imagine myself playing an exalted role of the insanely exalted role Carlos was fattening me for.

In a Shaft of Light The Prophet Concentrates on Everyone's Pain and Suffering, Everywhere.

Extremely juvenile, I know, but the game comforts me.

Carlos acts as if as if I'm no longer present. He makes donuts, cakes and pies early and phones realtors later, looking to buy a space that would combine living quarters for seven, hold activities for two hundred, and show off a glorious new bakery. Meaning whenever the subject of mortgages comes up, lo! the scales fall from his eyes.

He can see me again!

"How much have you got?" He means in addition to the business and the building. "No shit." He's squeezing my shoulders, basking in my presence. The mere mention of my more than $500K—left from my parents' "seed money" and the result of my never having gone anywhere or done anything but work in this shop—earns me a few hot moments of adulation.

He gives me a maddening, lingering caress. I still want him desperately, but unless we're talking down payments, Carlos is totally indifferent to me.

Since Carlos began ignoring my existence, I've been eating almost nothing. But tonight something happened. One moment I stood downstairs, staring at an Amaretto cheesecake. And the next, quivering from head to toe, I was allowing myself a little sliver…which, as it dissolved in my mouth, awakened an overwhelming need to go *on* allowing myself little slivers until the whole sweet rich thing was gone.

Dazed, almost drugged, I tromped upstairs, demanding he tell me what's wrong.

"Wrong?" Carlos shifted in his chair—my chair.

"Yeah, what's wrong?"

"Well, let's see." Staring at the ceiling, he tapped his temple. Then he made a frame with his fingers and squinted at me. "When you ask, what's wrong?" Carlos said, "are you inquiring about my health?"

About to walk away, I turned back. "You know what I mean."

"Or why I'm sitting here unable to read because the light's burned out?"

I retreated to the apartment's kitchen, but Carlos followed me. I put water on for tea. Carlos flashed me a loathsome smirk. Before long I gave in to the unremitting fury and said, "Okay, Carlos. Why, once you become my lover, do you hate me?"

And then his face went blank. A shadow passed and he stood silent. I turned off the stove, about to walk away, when he jumped in front and shoved me against the wall. In a grotesque voice, he parroted me: "How come? But why? What's the reason?"

I ducked past him but he grabbed my arm, which he twisted behind my back. When I struggled, he butted my head against the wall. The blow sounded a dull thud and produced an awful squish. The pain was shocking. Carlos let go; there was a string of stars; the hall light bulb swung from the ceiling. He was shaking his finger at me. "You—you deserved that! Nothing but whining and sniveling. When I've always done all the work, and you've socked away all the profits." Then he whirled back at me. "But the thing I really can't stand is that wheezy, sniffly sound you make when you breathe." Tendons throbbed from his neck. A vein pulsed on his forehead. "The sound of you chewing and glugging. The way you mewl around, with your fat fucking tongue hanging out of your fat fucking face."

This last had been punctuated by steps on the stairwell, which I hadn't noticed until Carlos shut up. We heard the knock-knock. Instantly in control, he raised his eyebrows to indicate, Was I going to answer that or what?

Woozy with pain, I opened the door to Maggie, who tapped me brightly on the chest with the fliers she had rolled up in her hand. Wrinkling her forehead, she said, "Oh, did I come at a bad time?"

The three of us shifted to the front room. Maggie said everywhere she went people were talking about Religion Without Rules. On campus, in town, everywhere. But the big news was, she'd found the perfect space for us, a defunct bowling alley, about ten miles west. At which point, I nodded and claimed I was going to bed.

*

Night Descends on the Baffled Prophet. Forsaken in his Room, He Awaits Another Dawn. The Walls Close In.

*

I could, it just occurred to me, take the money and run. With my five hundred thousand dollars in savings, I could go to California and join one of those Revelation/Apocalypse groups. I could travel the world, start a new business, whatever. ≈

Despite Everything

Last night marked the ninth meeting of Religion Without Rules. Not including the first two meetings, I do all the talking. Last night the crowd overflowed the shop. People milled about the sidewalk, while Bald Paul set up video outside. We reap more money all the time, which I find so disturbing, I just let Carlos handle it.

But when I mount the dais and face the crowd, I don't know, I just go into this mode that feels so fantastic, I'm amazed no one's tried to lock me up. (Yet.) ≈

Don't Look Down

March 21

I know now how it will go. If I close my eyes I can see the whole long dizzying trek into the future. Not all the way to the end exactly, but far enough to realize that whatever that is glinting off in the distance, it's inevitable. There's no changing it.

Everything I said at last night's meeting was true. I said: "You can't give up. No matter how often you pray for the experience—no matter how often you think you're there, it's finally, finally happening—only to discover that it was just a presage to transcendence and not the thing itself, you have to go on. You have to keep wanting it.

"Because," I said, "there is no alternative. Other than to spend your life blotting out basic questions. Ordering yourself to shut up, don't think! How are you going to suppress everything you wonder about? Everything you dream?"

"*Either*," I said, turning off the mike, my voice big with inherent reverb, "you're fiercely seeking a spiritual awareness that never comes, that almost comes, that fools you into believing it's almost, almost here, and then, after a second, evaporates. *Or,* you're floating aimlessly, eyes fixed on a monotonous white sky.

"What choice do you have?" I asked the crowd. "Are you who've suffered a thousand disappointments going to sink into a stuporous life, accumulating the most expensive junk you can find? A shiny machine, a glimmering stone, a nameplate? Your own true-life saga this week's reality show: You think *that* will make it all worth it? The same day you fulfill your desire, you discover it's not enough. You've got to have *more*! And then if it turns out, the thing you wanted so badly for so long makes you miserable, you're a step ahead. Because if it robs you of everything you've ever loved, at least you realize what a fool you were!

"But if, as also happens, the fame, money, power, knowledge, the beach house, just gets kind of old, kind of boring after a while, you'll let down your guard, and all the questions you tamp down, blot out, hush up—will erupt. The minute you relax, the minute you shut your eyes or skip your medication, they'll inundate you. All those silenced aspirations will deluge your mind.

"Ultimately, everyone prays to *someone*. In dire straits, we all ask, 'What *am* I doing here? And *why?*' Don't we?" I asked, spreading my arms. "Don't we *all?*"

The gauzy white shirt I was wearing filled the air. I raised my arms and the material colored the room, draping us with a soothing collective coolness.

"Whether we know it or not," I said, "we all beg for faith. Faced with mortal danger, atheists turn hopeful; fundamentalists doubt. In desperation, we all whisper, 'Dear God, please, keep the plane up; pull us out of this nosedive.' Of course, after the crisis, our prayers disperse. We jump head first into the mainstream. 'Who's going to win the championship, the election, the lottery?'

"Oh, maybe a few saints, manic-depressives, people on the brink of death can sustain spiritual awareness. But the rest of us have to stick to the here and now. We can't spend every second striving for what we can never, ever have. We have jobs to do.

"Right?" (Looking up I saw Stephanie and Maggie brandishing stacks of money.)

"Besides, it's really not up to us. There's no way we can *earn* a direct experience of God. There's no way we *deserve* it. It either happens or it doesn't. The best we can hope for, *if* we say the right words, *if* we kneel perfectly straight, is a shivery intuition. And even then, even then, we can only stand so much. Anything closer to the Divine than a gentle, invisible flutter, a welling in our chests, and we'd keel over and die.

"Right?" I said, spreading my arms. "Right?" And the air near my face shifted. My fingers tingled. My words went out to the audience and it was as if I touched each person in the room. My shirt billowed over their luminous, upturned faces. My words drew the people to me and I gathered their ravenous souls to my about-to-burst breast. I hugged them and cooed in their ears: "But that's okay. It's all right. For no matter how often the shiver, the bath of light, distant trumpet playing, the moment of levitation turn out to be just that and nothing more

—turn out, after a brief stab of ecstasy, to be a chill, a glare, the odd reception from a passing radio and not signs from heaven—we will *not* give up. We will joyfully embrace every glancing, passing shadow that comes our way. No matter how futile it seems. Right?

"Right?"

And then—shit—*I looked down!* ≈

PART TWO: Success Changes You

Better Than Sex

It's all that matters.

It's better than sex.

It's who I am. Why I'm alive.

It's music; it's dance; it's dross transmuting not just to gold, but more: through time and beyond, constantly sculpting it. No kidding.

Wednesdays now, and Saturdays, I stand on a stage at the Y or another community center, and on Tuesdays and Sundays, I hold court at the shop. For the moment, I have this incredible gift. It's not something I expected or worked for. It just happened. I bend, whisper, sing, shout—and a radiant light surrounds and then emanates from people. Outside the wind blows; waves crash upon the shore (and presumptuous as it sounds, I know), trees tremble and leaves and dust swirl about the streets. While inside, hearts and minds spring wide open. Pure and perfect souls burst from hardened husks.

You have to try it. Stand on a stage and spin what's uniquely inside you with what's truly *out* there. You can't go wrong. The giddy beauty and awful power come on their own. It's me and not me: You and not you: it is marvelous, unending flux. ≈

Tiptoeing

April 10

It's taken me a while to notice, so thrilled have I been, so wrapped up in my newfound skills—*but:* Carlos, Stephanie, Maggie and her "occasional boyfriend," Lyle (whose existence makes me sick with jealousy)—all treat me with a hesitant politeness and weird respect. Of course the regulars and newcomers are deferential. Last week, old Mr. Downey and old Mr. Hedlund actually declared they would *retroactively* pay full price! But I said, no, no, eighty percent from now on was plenty.

For a while there, Carlos played his mind-control games. But he's adjusting. After each show, he hugs me gently, tells me how fantastic I was, and always asks, *Can he do anything for me?* Would I like him to stick around?

"For what?" I laugh.

Once, after an especially ecstatic performance, I remember, Carlos kissing me and marveling in a choked voice. But oddly ever since, his presence, his gaze, and even his touch barely register with me. Only when I asked him to handle

RWR's finances, and of course, the shop's too, did we seem to be on the same wavelength.

"Are you sure?" Carlos asked. "Because, you know, I've got plans."

And I in my separate, all-absorbing little world, said, "Right. I know you've got plans. So hire an accountant."

The money, the crowds, the blinding *awe* envelop me. I have to calm down. Or else I'm too giddy to travel from here to there. And I do, after all, have business to attend to.

At six a.m., I bless the bread dough before an audience. Some thirty people show up to watch as I knead it vigorously for five or ten minutes. And then at ten a.m. and four p.m., I do this little benediction-thing where I drizzle chocolate on éclairs, which are then passed out to everybody in the store. The followers wait and watch while I eat mine first.

This evening, after the éclair and before dinner, I slipped up to the apartment to do the souped-up elliptical machine I bought last week. With all the metaphysical energy I've got resonating, I've decided to work on my cardio-vascular system before and after all performances. I'm starting to look pretty good.

The big change came the minute Carlos stopped force-feeding me. Right away, I dropped five, maybe even ten, pounds. I'm aware of my body and when Maggie knocks on the apartment door, flouncing in, to perch on the coffee table, I get flustered and blush.

"Don't mind me," she says. *"Breathe!"*

"What?"

"No need to suck it in anymore, Malcolm. You're starting to look almost normal. When someone gets that fat within a few weeks—I mean, hour by hour, gaining weight right in front of my eyes—maybe it likewise just melts off once you quit eating."

"Gee, thanks."

"You're welcome." Then she bounces up and clicks in her little high-heeled boots to stand facing me as I work the machine. Palms out, she says, "I'm here to say, I'm sorry. I know. I've been a jerk. And as of right now, I won't act like that."

"Oh yeah?"

"It's like we're *so amazed* at what you're doing, we don't know what to say."

"All I know is everybody's being nice to me for a change, and I *like* it."

"We need to treat each other as regular friends. At least, you and I do."

"All right," I nod. "I'll try."

"Everything's happening at once, and if we're not careful," Maggie says, "it's going to get fucked up before it even gets going."

"So we'll be careful."

"Except as a rule, none of us are careful types. That's my point," Maggie says. "Everyone's tiptoeing around when we should be yelling and screaming."

"Not me. I don't yell. I don't scream."

"Well, I do," Maggie said. "Which is exactly why you need me." ≈

Sublime Forces

Occasionally, I still panic. A momentary relapse. But once I'm *out* there, arms spread, hair streaming, Truth and Light lifting me up, up, up, I can do no wrong. Spiritually, I somersault as Sublime Forces play tag in my veins. And the crowd, whether in Skokie or Wicker Park, the De Paul area or the University of Chicago is right there *with* me. We're *all* laughing and crying with joy!

Sometimes I go too fast; I'm overcome from the start. But then, with a wince, if I concentrate, if I fix myself, I can get it back. Often, I focus on one person. Our eyes meet. There is a shiver. A sigh. I catch it and lose it, and then magically spin from my solar plexus. Who needs to say anything? The whole building, every floor and ceiling, beam and board, reverberates. "What else is there?" I ask on tiptoes, tears streaming down my burning, beatified face. "My Lord."

As everyone gathers his things and departs, money and more money floods in. ≈

For Real

Okay, so not every minute of every meeting is *that* sublime. Certain gestures and set arguments can dominate. Not to mention the ego rush: For now, I am very hot. Very high on my ordinary body. Who wouldn't be?

Everybody rushes in already stoked. Before they even sit down, they're half lit with the Ray of Light they need so bad, and that I'm so famous for giving so, so well! I open my mouth and they're ready to lie down, open up, no holds barred. We're naming abstractions, "spiritual enlightenment," "enduring faith." Hard to know how much is real, how much hysteria.

But what if I'm faking it? Even though I am on guard all the time! Watching for tricks of light, layered space, even as I'm getting off. Because everyone else flies into delirium as if never before.

"Faking it," I tell Carlos, "only has to happen once. Then it's part of the entire texture. The whole thing would be over."

"What are you talking about?"

"What scares me. You know, act euphoric and you feel euphoric."

"Malcolm, I've waited all my life for this! *Don't* get squeamish. Take a pill."

"If I wasn't a little scared, I don't think I could do it, Carlos."

"Where's Maggie?" he asks. "Talk to her. Because right now, I've got to work."

"Sure, but what you're setting up, the big financial picture, et cetera, scares me, too. What's happening with your projections, Carlos?"

"Oh please. I understand every factor here and I am *not* going to blow it."

"I want some idea, though. I want to meet the accountant."

"The accountant!" Carlos scoffs. "You are defining a sacred, transcendent realm—which four nights a week you share with all kinds of people, and you want to spend your days talking inflows and outlays with Herb Plochman?"

"Herb Plochman? That's a real guy?"

And Carlos steps back, holds his chin, grinning with delight. "Do you have *any* idea how much I love you, Malcolm?"

"Huh?"

"Filled with grace and as paranoid as ever." And then Carlos drapes his forearms over my neck. As enthralled as I've been, he hasn't run his hands down my back in weeks. If he was ever going to kiss my lips like he needed them to survive, you'd think he'd do it now.

But oh, he does more. He sinks to his knees and slips his head under my gown. Suddenly, Carlos is all mouth and rough tongue. ≈

The Tip of the Tip

1. The shop's closed this week.

2. Since it's being gutted.

3. So we can expand and renovate.

At the moment Mad—"What the fuck do I have to fucking do to get through to you fucking morons?"—Mike and his chain-smoking demolition crew are knocking down walls, ripping up floors. The sound of their saws alone—three circular metal-eaters—sends an oscillating circuit of pain through my teeth.

In less than a week Carlos has changed the map. He—I mean, we—have bought up all the property on the block. The dress shop, the dry cleaner, and the nail salon.

Two days of negotiating with the store owners, a twenty minute conversation with the town supervisor, and off we trotted, Carlos in suit and tie—his waist-length hair cut above his jawline!—and me in a sweater vest and chinos, to sit in a stuffy office above a pet food store: Carlos and I, Fletcher and Franklin Brazil, our bodybuilding, identical twin lawyers (who are also representing the store owners, and the banks), Matt Kessler, the dry cleaner, Shari Murtaugh of Amelia's Dress Shop, and Sylvia Sloane of Sylvia's Custom Nail Wraps. We passed thirty-six documents around the table and signed our names on hundreds of dotted lines. And still, every two seconds Franklin or Fletcher would jump up and point at one of us. "Sign here. Sign here. Sign here." Everything in triplicate.

I would have thought, This can *not* be happening; I am not signing my life away. I am *not* borrowing two million dollars!

Except—it took all my concentration just to breathe, or rather, *not* to breathe. Fletcher and Franklin seemed locked in competition as to which one was more awash in cologne. Carlos's hair gel lay greenish and thick on his slick new 'do (which doesn't look right at all!) Sylvia Sloane shuddered and chomped on butterscotch candies. And Matt Kessler radiated the smell of cleaning fluid so powerfully you could almost see the toxic blue rays glowing from his head. Also swirling in the unventilated air were the eternal residues of cigarettes and alcohol as well as fresh horrible gusts of drilled-away tooth matter and amalgam from the dentist's office across the hall.

Of course I could also smell myself—the smell of anxiety worse than anxiety, the smell of me borrowing two million dollars and tying my fate to Carlos's forever!

He kept hissing at me, "Would you relax?"

Meanwhile, Shari Murtaugh, the pixyish woman in her sixties sitting on the other side of me, was showing me a little picture of the Virgin, even as the paper-signing continued apace. She slid closer, resting her fingertips on my shoulder. "I haven't been to one of your meetings yet," she whispered, "but, if I didn't have it on the highest authority how saintly you are, I would never sell you my dress shop. Never."

I started to say thank you, except was "thank you" the right response? Instead I sat dumbfounded with the holy picture in my palm. Was it a gift? Or was I supposed to have handed it back a minute ago already?

Seeing my confusion, Shari nodded at me brightly. "Go ahead, Father."

Father? "Oh no. No. Call me Malcolm. Malcolm is fine."

There was this terrible air of expectancy and embarrassment. Because I still didn't know: Was I supposed to kiss the picture? Press it to my forehead? Or, forehead, chest, left shoulder, right? (Up until puberty I was an unquestioning Catholic.)

"It's okay to put it in your pocket," Shari Murtaugh said. "When She bleeds, it doesn't stain. It doesn't even get wet, really."

I must have looked stricken. And doubtful. I may have let out a gasp.

"It's guaranteed authentic," she said, "from that shrine in New Jersey."

"Yes…" I managed to smile weakly and put the thing in my pocket.

And I noticed Carlos heave with relief. Like: *Phew! Thank God! Close one.*

From this vantage point (over the din of Mad Mike's

demolition) I can hear what I *almost* heard when we were signing all those papers: Carlos admonishing me: Don't blow this. We're talking a chain of bakeries, a franchise. He practically jiggled his fist in an abbreviated thumbs up, *ye-es-sss.*.

In any case, once it was clear I was more afraid of offending Shari Murtaugh than of losing everything I had, Carlos and company knew the deal was sealed. No matter how many more signatures were needed, no matter how high the closing costs, whatever the interest rates or points. Shari Murtaugh was assured I wasn't fraudulent—I'd passed the bleeding holy card test—and I had demonstrated that hurting a fetishist's feelings bothered me more than paying half a million dollars for a dress shop.

Outside, we all shook hands. Matt and Shari and Sylvia got into a black Cadillac. Off, they said, to celebrate. Fletcher and Franklin waved ta-ta, lumbering off to their gym. Carlos and I looked around. The empty street was ours. His warm, sinewy arm around my shoulders, he pulled punches to my chin and chest, and said, "You did it! Cosmic opportunity hovered just out of reach but you rose to meet it."

And suddenly, Carlos's breath felt soft and warm in my ear. "Of course, the main thing, the exciting thing, is the *spiritual* aspect. The spiritual street is wide open. It's boundless territory." He pulled me over to the nail salon and pressed me up against the entrance. A canvas awning covered our heads. He ran his hands up and down my anorak. He took my face in his hands and electricity fused us together. We stood in a column of light. There was a rush, a beating of wings—and then a jolt—What was I doing? What had just happened?

After weeks of awkwardness, Carlos and I stood wrapped in an ecstatic embrace in the doorway of Sylvia's Custom Nail Wraps. We shook ourselves simultaneously and began to speak simultaneously. "Did you—" "Are you—" We laughed. We wiped our eyes. We gazed at one another.

And following long, drifting seconds, Carlos whispered, "This is just the beginning, Malcolm."

To which I added, "The tip of the tip." ≈

A Beautiful Boy

April 16

Mad Mike and his bleary, bad-tempered crew are on their eighty-eighth coffee break. They're all bloated and grizzled, except one, Tyler, who's young and beautiful. Hauntingly beautiful. Scary-young.

Huddled in the corner, the crew smokes hollowed out cigars filled with home-grown. The beautiful Tyler doffs his beret, releasing a cascade of dark curls. He slinks and turns, feigning a movie star's scowl as his hammer-heavy belt slips down his hips. The other guys spit and scratch. I can't believe how they act! As if oblivious to him!

My beloved shop, meanwhile, is a bombed-out shell of pulverized plaster. Layers of smoke undulate in the air. My eyes burn. My throat hurts. I can't stay here and I absolutely cannot leave.

Have I mentioned how much more weight I'm losing? Lately it seems everything of substance makes me gag. I am chronically nauseated and ravenous, both. ≈

At Least, Apparently

April 17

Just before he left today, the boy Tyler sauntered over and offered me a hit of home-grown. I said no thanks, and he leaned closer, asking if I minded. The soul of concern, of sweetness, light, peace, joy and hope, he asked: was it okay with me? I shrugged and he rocked back in his shiny rubber boots and gave me a smile that made me start as if I'd scalded my tongue.

Burning with alarm, I raced up here and jumped in the shower, which, because of the plumbing work, was ice cold. But cold water was not enough: I needed noise and distraction. So, I sang old hits at the top of my lungs. An inner voice, however, does not need to shout. It's got a volume all its own. I twisted and turned, trying to hold it back. But the voice was already broadcasting my every thought, deeper, louder inside my head.

So what choice did I have?

Name it and tame it. Say it out loud.

Here goes: Up close and smiling, this boy Tyler reminds

me a little of my long-dead, first-and-only-one-who-counts
lover Colin. More than a little. A lot. ("Why all the uproar?"
Colin asked once. "It's so futile.")

"Because they're wrong and I'm right. Give me a minute
and I can prove it."

"No, you can't," Colin had said. "And besides, you don't
get a minute, ever. No one does."

Why the fuck isn't he here? He fell-jumped-flew off a roof
as I watched and I need him more now than ever. Young and
rash, we basked in more love than anyone else could possibly
fathom. I'm not exaggerating. As a spiritual leader, I recognize
typical human limits. The way Colin and I worked? We were so
far there, you can't know. Imagine perfect unity and give up.
Maybe you can come up with the barest shadow of a shadow of
what we felt. Colin and I were beyond the world. Beyond life
and death, which is why, so what if he died six years ago? I
need him, and anything as ultimately mundane and inescapable
as *death* is no excuse! The guy's abandoned me. At least,
apparently. ≈

Momentum or Die

As of last week, even before Mad Mike and company started demolishing the shop, I agreed to start doing seven meetings a week, at Y's, conference halls, corporate headquarters, downtown clubs, you name it. Maggie does the bookings. One night I'm in a run-down, hundred year old building on State Street, with ancient gray carpeting, orange plastic seats, and the smell of microwave popcorn permeating the air. Another night I'm addressing a bunch of ad execs at the Marriott. Some nights, I speak to a few hundred people, other nights a few dozen. I do my little shows in library discussion rooms and Methodist conference halls, basement bingo parlors, and yesterday afternoon, in the stately home of the woman presiding over the Kenilworth Beautification Association.

I used to think that possibly Carlos was right—I have a special gift, but lately, seven nights a week, I have to wonder if it makes a bit of difference what I do or say. I've promised Carlos I will keep going until we're financially unassailable. Or at least "not unstable."

Meanwhile, he is in the process of buying three new bakeries, where I can extend the blessings of the bread and benedictions of the chocolate éclairs.

"And who," I ask, "is negotiating these purchases?"

"Fletcher and Franklin and I."

"Really."

"I *know* about real estate, Malcolm. I know this city. I know what I'm doing. And I've waited all my life for this, okay?"

"Oh, me too," I say as Maggie taps off her phone.

"Next Tuesday," she says, "Oak Park Town Hall Theater, eight o'clock."

"You know, when I was a little boy," I tell them, "and people asked me what I wanted to do when I grew up? I always said: dash about a great, big rented conference room, lift my billowy shirt, and show everybody my wounds."

"Are seven meetings a week," Maggie wonders, "too much?"

"No," Carlos says. "Don't get all cynical and self-critical, Malcolm. You're doing great. It's easy for you—anybody can see that! Besides, this is the crucial time. We either build momentum now or interest will fade. I know! I've been through this before: If we don't keep growing, we'll die." ≈

Pure and Total

Today is my twenty-seventh birthday. No, April 20th was my twenty-seventh birthday but it's also Adolph Hitler's hundred and twelfth birthday, which is why my mother insists my actual DOB was the day I was *due,* not the evil dawn at which I prematurely arrived.

This morning, I recalled reading in an astrology book that those born on April 20th can, when speaking to crowds, project an extraordinary power over them. Isn't that stupid? What astrological addendum goes to those born on Hitler's birthday? *'If you don't watch yourself, you might murder six million people?'*

So whenever I start wondering if I could be one of the genuine prophets, double my idiocy, why doncha? I can't take this. My head aches. The shop's in ruin. Everywhere I look everything is pure and total shit. ≈

Family

For my birthday, Maggie hopped up and down, saying, "Here's my gift, Malkie. Open it first." The box she gave me came from the Nature Company, and as I started to shake it, she jumped up, "Careful. It's alive. Dormant but—" She turned around, crossed her fingers, and whispered, "Oh God don't let me spoil the surprise."

I untied the ribbon, lifted the lid, and she said, "It's for when the shop is finished. Outside, in the back, I thought we'd plant a garden."

It was a kit for raising butterflies. "Thank you," I said.

"They had one for hummingbirds too," Maggie said. "But I don't know, I liked the idea of butterflies better."

My parents called from Carmel, California, on speaker-phone so they could both talk at once. Did I get my birthday present? Yes, I said, the briefcase was beautiful.

"Coming up in the world!" my father declared.

"It's not that we're not proud," my mother said, her voice

wavering. "It's just that, that we worry. No one can have all the answers. And you…you really do tend to go overboard."

"So," my father thundered, "how does it feel to be pushing thirty?"

"Lucas, twenty-seven is not pushing thirty! Malcom's in his mid-twenties. Honey, we really want to see you."

"Well, we're in the middle of construction…"

"So tell us when's a good time."

"Okay, I will."

"Nothing like family," Stephanie said. "Your face is the color of marinara sauce."

"You have to get over that," Carlos said. "We're self-made. That's what sets us apart. *We're* your family now. Where we come from, how we were brought up—none of that matters any more."

"Can we talk about something else?"

Then Carlos gave me a gold neck chain with RWR in the center.

"Very tasteful," I said. "Very apt. Thank you."

"RWR" Carlos said, fixing the chain on my neck. "It's so perfect."

"Unpronounceable, though. I think it's better when you can say the acronym like a word."

"Oh, well," he said, determined not to seem miffed.

God, I was tired. It's terrible when Carlos is sincere. But as I sat there, with the thing around my neck, he got not just sincere but sincerely soap opera. *Carlos!* He kissed my hand and said—in front of Maggie—that I was his *prince!* (Of course

Stephanie was also there, but being waitress extraordinaire, she somehow conveyed that she hadn't really heard us.)

I laughed—couldn't help it.

"All right," Carlos said. "Be like that." He stomped into the kitchen, made himself a gin and tonic and drained it in front of us.

Then he brought the gin and tonic bottles to the table and mixed himself another one. "We do not conform," he said, "to designated strata."

"We're beyond demography," Maggie said. (She's *so* good with him and *so* good with me. Where would I be without her?)

"Well, my family life," Stephanie said, *her* face red now, "has improved fantastically this year. It's the extra money—I find I can buy a little time, and a little freedom. I can make my sister's life a little less sad." Stephanie put a hand on my shoulder, kissed my cheek, and handed me a flat, sky-blue box.

More jewelry from Tiffany's? *Oh!* It was a simple silver picture frame, five by seven, with a photograph of me six years ago, young, handsome, dazed and grief-stricken, in front of the shop my parents had just bought for me.

"Where did you get this?"

"I took it one afternoon after my shift."

"One afternoon a long, long time ago," I said, feeling touched and tearful. ≈

Doubt

*E*very seat is taken. I have to stand on stage and say what I believe.

I can't go on—it's over! Because here's the catch: I really do have to believe what I say. At last night's meeting—after nonstop weeks—tired, bored, fed up—I found myself impersonating a doltish school teacher. I blinked and sighed. "Pencils sharp? Erasers ready—" I looked around, hand shielding my eyes, and said, "Well, what have we here? A test of faith!"

Silence.

"Any thoughts?"

Silence.

"Anyone?"

I waited and waited a few beats more. "Well then," I said, "Why don't we come back to that later. How about an easy one? Like the meaning of life, sex, and death?"

The participants sat glassy eyed and dumb.

"Now come on, class. What do we think we're doing here?"

There were giggles.

"Want me to tell you?"

"Yeah, tell us," a woman in the back called out. "Tell us *something*." I think it was my friend Bailey. Beaming recognition, I asked her to stand up. And then I forgot the question. Finger to my chin, I said, "Where was I?"

And the audience laughed. Bailey (or someone who looks just like her) said, "The meaning of life, sex, and death."

"Oh right, right! I know that one." More laughter. "It's simple really, just hard to describe." I scratched my head. It's... it's, right on the tip of my tongue..." I played the idiot. Fun, fun, fun! The take topped three thousand, our best yet. ≈

What Do I Care

I left the stage twelve hours ago; I go back on tonight. Am I frightened? Mortified? Exhausted? *I am a void—personified!*

Except you can no longer tell from the outside. My almighty, anonymous needs still rage. The shop's closed, the kitchen's gutted. All those tarts and strudels, cheesecakes, brownies and donuts don't exist at the moment. And maybe because I wear the muslin gown as much as he wants (or else I was so *easy* he lost interest), Carlos has no renewed interest in what I eat or drink.

And my routine has changed. I take long walks alone. This morning as I crossed the Plaza del Lago shopping mall, Carlos appeared, silently, coolly in sync with me. We traversed the small terrace and he stroked my left side. We leaned into a brick corner and he hoisted me a bit in the air. And I, reeling with desire and distaste, writhed, resisted, and succumbed. All the while inadvertently catching the eye of a woman loading groceries into a green Volvo. She shrugged and smiled.

I twisted my head and wiggled my hands, signaling her:

this is *not* what it looks like. The woman slammed her car door and comically saluted. Was she saying, "I know; I've been there"? Or was it, "What do I care?"

And then it hit me that that's my perennial question: what do *I* care? Anytime anyone misunderstands me, I'm ready to die. My life seems to depend on getting the population at large to take my side. ≈

Homeless

May 19

Carlos is out securing hotel rooms for us for the next few weeks. The shop and its bought-out neighbors are totally gutted. I can either pace through the wreckage as I have for hours, or I can tap on my laptop as I am now. Either way, my presence is negligible. Either way, whether i stay or go—out for a drink, a walk, maybe along the lake, whatever: *Everything everywhere is crashing all around me!*

Everything's packed but the sound system. Gregorian chants of Benedictine monks fill my bare, crate-stacked rooms. How long since I've eaten solid food? Naked in front of the mirror, I can feel my ribs.

So okay, I admitted it weeks ago! Tyler reminds me of Colin! Now can I get dressed? Now will I be able to eat? Or if not eat—thinking of him (them) my skin feels so tight—I can at least drink: I'll start with what's left of Carlos's gin. And then, when that's not enough, for how could it be? I'll head downtown to see if the bar where Colin and I used to drink, illegally underage, still exists.

*

Colin and I used to come here on weekends; Sammy's was the only place that didn't card us. Now everything except the name has changed. Something about the lighting back then, plus, I think, a mechanism in the floor, created an illusion of speed. A lush female impersonator played the piano and sang bawdy old blues songs while the whole place seemingly hurtled through space. Now the light is steady and bright enough for reading. The music is piped in, and really, pretty much white noise. Predictable, insipid changes or not, the strangest thing about wandering into Sammy's is how unstrange it is. How unexpectedly normal it makes me feel.

I'm finishing a spanakopita platter—Sammy's Greek food stayed on the menu—when Carlos calls me from the Swiss Crown Hotel. He's booked us for two weeks in a suite costing —"You don't want to know, Malcolm."

"Oh, really? *That* much."

"We need it, so we can work; so we can think." (*Oh well*, in that case…)

Which reminds him—he's bought himself some clothes. "Nondenominational has its privileges." (Right.)

"Wait 'til you see this place, Malcolm. The view is incredible!"

(I bet.) But I've still got one more night before Mad Mike and company rip out and haul away the last wall and floor board of my only home.

"Maggie will pick you up. Where are you?"

*

Carlos the maestro-provocateur rolls up the cuffs of his gorgeous new celadon shirt and, pressing me from behind, clasps his hands over my belt. "Look at the view," he whispers, resting his chin on my shoulder. But for once I shake him off. The view is everywhere you look. All brilliant, thrashing Lake Michigan in one direction; all shining city in the other: the suite's walls are solid glass. ≈

Swiss Crown Suites 3601-3602 (week 2)

June 5

1. Without my store

2. Without my home

3. My life has no structure

4. MY LIFE HAS NO MEANING! ≈

Why?

1. Why was I born?

2. Why am I alive?

3. Why, I have no fucking idea. $\approx$

The Masquerade Is Over

I hate it here. The environment is so artificial, so studiously deluxe but not offensively grand. It's a glass-walled prison, high in the sky. The hotel staff buzzes about, concerned and busy, and quick to defer to the tiniest alteration of my mood.

"It's a fucking fish tank," I complain to Carlos, who then informs me the construction on the Linden Street shop is stalled.

"Some kind of fuck-up with Mad Mike's shipper," Carlos says. "And a few problems with variances."

"Meaning?"

"Meaning we stay here another two weeks," Carlos says, "give or take."

"Five weeks in the Swiss Crown?"

"The shop in Lincoln Park opens in a few days. Stephanie wants to manage it, and the prospects look very promising."

"I don't know," I tell him, dejected by his 'promising prospects.' "Past a certain point—taking this long, costing this much—it's not worth it."

"The money?" (I didn't mean the money.) "You're worried about the money, Malcolm? Christ! Just do the éclair thing in the mornings, at every new shop. That'll cover the hotel bill."

"That's twice a day at the shop in Bucktown, twice in Wicker Park, and twice in Lincoln Park, right? Old Orchard. Northbrook. On top of the regular meetings, the shows."

"That's right," Carlos says. "Think of them as shows. Easy gigs, as natural as breathing. That's how good you are. Just go out, sing and dance like a trouper, and tend to your quivering little ego later. I'm negotiating with some people now about a book, a Doctrine, if you will. *That's* where your real life, real beliefs will come out, and you'll be able to relax."

"I don't think so, Carlos. I want to get out."

"Will you stop? Everything's going great. Two, three more weeks you'll be home, and all this disorientation, all the *work*, and showmanship, will be more than worth it. Way more! Why, half the money coming in is going right back out to work for us."

"What do you mean?"

"I'm investing it. You've got to pay yourself before you pay creditors; we want that money *working* for us."

"Carlos, if you're talking about stocks, tell me you have some good advisors."

"Strictly blue chip," he says. "Nothing fancy. A few mutual funds. But even in this market, if we set up one branch in Europe, one in the Caribbean maybe, South America, we can retire."

(Is Carlos stupid? I never thought he was stupid. He acts so smart. He's gotta be kidding.) "Will you show me the books?"

"Of course," he says. "I'll show you anything you want, anytime you want. Just so you understand upfront that very temporarily, what with all the new stores and keeping the suites for a couple of weeks, we're going to have some heavy outlays."

"So you need me to do the bread and éclair thing at five— or is it seven—new stores? Twice a day, each day, on top of the meetings."

"It's not that much, Malcolm. I mean if you think about it, it's a hell of a lot easier than most jobs!" (I wish you could see his face, how instantly Carlos goes from reproving appraiser to ardent lover.) "God, I love you!" he rasps, eyes on high beam as he slithers over to hug me. "Oh," he says, his voice choked, his gaze hot and skin flushed, "You are such a pure and perfect soul!" Carlos can really turn it on and off. Tell me I never bought his shit, though. He's not just transparent. Ridiculous. So, you know, I laugh.

"Oh, I know," he says, shaking his head. "For you it's this big joke. When I've been dying for you—really dying. You've no fucking idea how hard it was to get through all these years, keeping my need for my boss under wraps. I mean," Carlos says, "here you are, sexiest thing in the world, out of my league, but *not* out of reach. And I maintain. I play my part."

It's preposterous. He's not playing it right—so overt and abrupt. But, dumb, needy me. I step closer to him. Carlos takes my head in his hands, and the sheer nerve! Once he's sure I've noticed how dark and liquid, how reflective and shining his eyes are, he dips his face to my chest, and pleads into my shirt. "Malcolm, you've no idea how bad I want you. And it *never* lets up. It kills me."

"If it really killed you, it'd be over." And he looks so shocked, so stung, I can't help it: I let him win; I let him lead me into Suite 3601's blue bedroom. Locking the door, he mews into my neck and peels off my clothes. Except first, I lay down a stipulation: we switch positions. Today, since I'm the top in real life (well, I *am*, aren't I?) I'll take the bottom in sex, and as he in real life is beneath me (this *is* the way it is) he'll take the top.

And right away the reversal feels new and fantastic. The whole sexual act is scream-out-loud thrilling. I thrash and cry —it's scary how good it feels! And yet, and yet—this is the amazing thing: A minute afterwards I'm miraculously in-different. I can take Carlos, I can leave him; I really don't care.

≈

The Soul of Concern, of Sweetness, Light, Peace, Joy and Hope

June 20

Ten days later and I am still indifferent to Carlos. In fact I am indifferent to everyone and -thing except: one hopelessly unrealistic hope. For ever since my sweet, quickening encounter with the beautiful boy Tyler, when he so innocently and sincerely asked, *did I mind?* (Did I mind if he and his friends smoked ganja on my time?) I can think of nothing else! Every three seconds he's back, the soul of concern, of sweetness, light, peace, joy and hope, swaying politely in front of me, Blunt in hand.

I cannot concentrate. I cannot eat or sleep. I'm so fixated on that tool belt that seems to be wearing him more than he's wearing it. In my mind it's slowly sliding off of him, and I can't decide which I want more: to pull it up or down.

Tyler, Tyler, Tyler! If anything else matters, I don't care. Or remember. ≈

Disconnected

I skim the plans for Stephanie's store, on Belden in Lincoln Park, which she wants to manage with her new (first in all the years I've known her) boyfriend, Rafe Hardeway.

I wait and hope and pray, and this morning I tell Carlos—again—he can do what he wants with the money. I can't keep my mind on it.

"You can't keep your mind on it?"

"I don't know how else to explain it. It bores me—and worries me—to the point where I'd rather not think about it."

"Well, we are investing a little more aggressively," he says. "We're looking at a couple of high-yield funds."

"We?"

"Herb Plochman and me," Carlos says. "And of course we've still got Fletcher and Franklin working for us."

"See, this is what makes me anxious: Fletcher and Franklin and Herb Plochman."

"Leave them to me," Carlos says, "I know what their limitations are and I know how to handle them. All you need to know is that our next step will probably be to convert a few big-name, big-money donors."

"We're in trouble, aren't we?"

"Anything but," Carlos says.

Carlos and I may have an on-again, off-again connection. But for now it's *completely* off. I'm standing here looking at him, and it's as if a hundred miles separates us. "What about your art?" I ask him. "Your baking?"

He shrugs, waves a hand, "Ffuh..."

"Well, then, what about your quest?"

And he hoots. "My *'quest'*?"

"You know..." Taken aback by Carlos's allegiance to money over all else, I press: "Faith versus doubt—stuff like that." ≈

Drifting

I will never get out. The clouds out the windows roll forward and back like infinitely big car wash brushes. I'm a blank, a lump, a foam rubber mound on a brocade zephyr. And nothing will ever change. ≈

Whatever You Categorically Deny Yourself Categorically Rules You

June 24

I saw him! At the Amphitheater tonight, in mid-performance, I pivoted, my arm swooping down, my voice rising, "You have to admit how you feel! You have to risk making mistakes and be prepared to pay for them," and there he was, his beautiful young face shining out from the dim and bobbing masses. Oh! If only I'd acted on my words! How *I* feel, what *I* want! Why didn't I jump down, walk arms outstretched to where he sat, and implore him? *Come with me!*

Instead, I fluttered. Shuddered, staggered, raked my hands through my hair and mopped my face with my billowy sleeve. "Forget sexual denial," I yelled, suddenly full of ire. "The nonsexual ideal is a fundamentalist lie! Banning sex leads not to enlightenment, not to purity, but to seething resentment and bitterest intolerance. Do not let the self-righteous and their festering superstitions oppress you!"

I could no longer see Tyler, but knowing he was there my voice sounded naked, my words indulgent and idiotically emphatic. "They object to people having sex because *they're* squeamish. And so I'm asking, isn't total preoccupation with abstinence just as vulgar as its opposite?

"Whatever you categorically deny yourself categorically rules you. These guys are obsessed with sex. To where they just can't fathom that sex is not the only thing.

"Or wait—wait a minute. Maybe…now that I mention it…maybe sex *is* the only thing. Maybe whatever you want more than anything, so that you get sick if you have to go without it—whatever it is that drives you, that directs your every endeavor in life—that thing is, for you, tantamount to sex."

Hitting a low note, I inadvertently let my stomach out and loosened the sash. Drawing myself up, up—Tyler was out there—I knotted it for all to see. I smiled (See, I'm human), and even gaily said, "There, now it won't come undone."

And, "As I was saying: If an experience such as eating an éclair, waking in a tub of tepid water, or getting stung by a bee reaches a certain intensity, a certain ratio of pleasure to pain, involving your entire consciousness, it is *ipso facto* sexual. But if it somehow goes further than that, beyond the sexual, beyond the personal, it becomes a *spiritual* experience."

At the word "spiritual," I rose higher, the light that surrounds me on stage glowing warmer, milkier. I reached out my hands as if to touch the boy's supernaturally beautiful face, which gazed luminously, gloriously up at me, from five rows in, two seats left of center.

"In which case, maybe those fundamentalists," I spoke

directly to him, "proscribe sex because it looks—and some-times, though how would they know, even feels—so much like prayer.

"Not that sex is always pleasurable. I mean, we've all had our hideous realizations—what have we done? We think something's going to be great and it turns out stupid and dull. *We're* dull and stupid—we're fakes."

I wanted Tyler to know: this magnetism is temporary. A vaudeville number, a spiel, a performance. It's not me, really. *"I am just like you,"* I said, and instantly realized my mistake. "I am just like you. We are the same. Not different." And—

Shit. I didn't need to look. I already knew: He was still there but gone from my field of vision. I was aware of him listening, but the brilliant face, so miraculously clear among the blur of anonymous heads, winked and went out, became in the blink of an eye another dot in one of the endless rows of amorphous bliss.

I am just like you. Why did I speak the words in my mouth instead of my heart? I bowed and turned—and when I looked up, he'd become invisible. The crowd was a sea of faces, a field of spots against the all-encompassing darkness.

"So okay, maybe I *can* imagine how total abstinence might look like the shortest, surest path to holiness…" I blah blah blahed.

Why didn't I go to him, take his hand, and lead him away to someplace safe and secluded? What if I missed my only chance; there's no going back?

Angry and scared—of myself and the boy Tyler, and of my past and bungled present—I veered off track. My powers abandoned me; the magic evaporated, and I heard myself ranting about my childhood religion.

"The Catholic priests—" yes, I resorted to talking about the priests!—"claim they're above erotic love. They refuse to admit their human desires, and thus too often succumb to an inhuman "aberration"—a priestly word for blacking out; for falling into a monstrous spell in which they rape some child. After which, I can just hear the priest telling the boy: 'Whatever you think just happened, did *not* happen. It's a sin to think such a thing, and a worse sin—a mortal sin—to speak of it. Trust in me,' the priest says, making the Sign of the Cross over the kneeling child's head, 'trust in God. Some boys,' the priest whispers through a gate he's made, fingers over his mouth, 'are special, favored.' He blows a kiss off his fingertips, 'Till next week then, *nothing happened.*'

"Of course when the boy goes home and looks in the mirror, he is one of them now; he belongs to the initiate…"

Afterwards, in the wings, a bigger throng than usual pressed in on me. They clapped and murmured, "Thank you, thank you." "Malcolm, Malcolm." You'd think I'd get used to it, but no. The crux of my being is exposed. It's grotesque and unseemly, and after a big public spillover, I want to hide in a dark, empty room. Except last night, upon seeing the boy Tyler, the sadness pooled deeper and deeper, while all the while a wall of hands patted my back and shoulders, head and chest.

Stephanie and her new boyfriend Rafe, Maggie and her trumpet-playing boyfriend Lyle, Louie and his girlfriend

Demetria, Professors Llewlleyn and Smith, the people I *knew*, clamored for special attention, kisses and handholding. I noticed Carlos at the top of the staircase. He mouthed "home run" and shook a loosely formed wrist at waist level, a crude promise of a vulgar reward. Bitter disgust welled, bringing fresh tears. Please God, *let me find the boy and get him out of here!* I kept slogging through the whirlpool, past Shari and Sylvia, Franklin and Fletcher, various erstwhile customers, students, shopkeepers and construction workers, searching for him.

Surely *the soul of concern, of sweetness, light, peace, joy, and hope* was close. I could feel him; he was waiting for me but—I could not reach him. I could not see him. Tyler was near. He was here and then—

Too late. ≈

Swiss Crown Suites 3601-3602, 3605-3607 (week 7)

July 9

Carlos, with yet another totally transforming haircut (clipped close and kept gray), strides through our combined celestial white suites in clothes that cost the earth; on a phone that's invisible in or out of his now-naked ear.

The rooms are glass, floor to ceiling. Altocumulus rows undulate around us. A Mogul for the Ages. (That's him.) Master of the Religion Without Rules. (That's me.)

I sit in new white clothes, festooned to an enormous white couch that Maggie and I bought yesterday. My pulse beats beneath a silk collar band. It runs in a searing swath from my navel to my groin. I can't swallow. I can't breathe.

I'm supposed to be composing the *RWR DOCTRINE*. The meetings have become weird and exhausting. I go on, say my stuff, people clap and cheer and money rises like mountains. Except, Carlos contends, not quite enough money; not at this juncture. "We've got to hit big, and follow hard with brand extensions." So my personal trainer and ally, Maggie, sits opposite me, also in new white clothes (involving, as always with her, plenty of deep cleavage), culling "significant concepts" from a file of meeting highlights. Or that's what she's supposed to be doing. Actually, she's texting with Stephanie and Rafe, who are in the middle of a grand opening in Lincoln Park.

Apparently I signed leases and hiring agreements. "You picked out the floor and ceiling tile with me. Remember? And you insisted on a limited menu. Six kinds of bread, three kinds of donuts…"

Head aching, I send e-mail from my laptop to hers, from the couch to the chair.

I can't do this!

"Don't be ridiculous," Maggie says, scrolling through her contacts and calling Carlos, who's perpetually on his phone: "Hey, Carlos, we need to talk. In the bedroom."

Hey Maggie—I'm consumed by humiliation,
wracked by guilt,
filled with dread

"Don't be silly," she says.

I can't do this!

"Of course you can. Right, Carlos?"

He swings through the suite, looking super-austere in his luxe tailoring and radically short hair. And as he bends to whisper in my ear, "Just stay focused, Malcolm. Put down what you think. What you—"

"I know, I know, I know already! What I *believe*."

"Exactly." Hand on my shoulder, Carlos claims he's within a hair's breadth of negotiating a publishing deal. "A best-seller, yes, they get that part, but what's harder for them to grasp is that first and foremost we're talking—" he raises an eyebrow, holds up a finger—"*sacred text*."

"Ha ha, Carlos." I slump deeper into the silk couch.

"Lighten up, Chuckles." He pats my cheek. "It's not the end of the world."

Maggie sighs and bows, motioning for Carlos to follow her into the bedroom. They mumble furiously for what seems like forever. At one point Maggie says, "Don't be such an asshole," and Carlos snaps, "Keep your voice down." ≈

Pigeon

We've taken four new suites. The better to keep the money and presents from all the lay-down-your-life-for-me hangers-on. While I stare listlessly at the interminable sky, Carlos and Maggie and a retinue of consultants bicker, prescribing this, proscribing that. Three RWR bakeries are up and running already, but not the real bakery, my home. It's nowhere near done, and nowhere near recognizable.

On top of which: The boy Tyler is nowhere to be found. Carlos, I just discovered, fired Mad Mike and his crew three and a half weeks ago.

"Mad Mike," Carlos adjusts a tiny earpiece, "is a drug addict. You think I want a cokehead working the rotary saws?" Carlos looks like someone from another life now, Carlos as CEO, Carlos in Brioni clothes. But he still finds time each day to sidle next to me and whisper, "You can do it," sometimes adding, "Pigeon."

Carlos has taken to calling me Pigeon, and I do not deign to notice.

I've promised myself to say nothing to him about the boy Tyler. The less Carlos knows about *the soul of concern, sweetness, light, peace, joy, and hope,* the better. ≈

My Candy-Red Heart

Jesus, I tell myself, put *something* down. Don't worry about DOCTRINE, that's ridiculous. Try making a list.

Okay—

> *Dread and confusion*
> *Uncontrollable suffering*

No, wait. Start over.

> POSSIBLE ASPECTS OF SO CALLED MYSTICAL
> EXPERIENCES:
> *Dread and confusion.*
> *Uncontrollable suffering.*
> *Unbounded joy.*
> *An acute awareness of time and timelessness—*

Apparently someone ordered room service. Maggie and Carlos are in the other room, on their phones. I call for them, but they don't answer. So after the bellhop lifts the lids off the dishes, I sign for them.

Still fasting, still pure, clean and resolute, I position the trolley of mineral water and chocolates, prosciutto and melon at the far end of the room, but not without marveling long and hard at the luscious rosettes of satiny pink tenderloin…Then it's back to "possible aspects:"

> *An acute awareness of time and timelessness—interacting.*
> *A milky vision of light—*

There's a tureen of poached pears, a boat of vanilla-ginger sauce.

> *A milky vision of light streaming from all things.*

Carlos paces and bargains; Maggie's trying to reach someone: "Hello? Hello?"

Tense, bored, but mostly just plain drained, I get up for a glass of water. Pour San Pellegrino into a crystal goblet and then—naturally they're *Godiva* chocolates—get an intense whiff of longing. I'm holding the powdery little chocolate ball up to my nose when Maggie yells from the other room, "Hey Slim! Hold on. I'll be there in a minute."

And I—quick—take the tiniest little bite.

And, no harm done, a minuscule bite or two more.

Before succumbing to all six bittersweet truffles.

Then it's straight to work on the *DOCTRINE*. One *DOCTRINE* coming right up.

But my hands are shaking.

To clear my head, I sample the other delicacies. Prosciutto and honeydew, luscious petals of beef, a poached pear covered with lighter-than-air *crème anglaise*.

I haven't eaten in weeks, no solid food for days, and these bolts of nourishment have set me thrumming. A sheen from each infusion forms on my skin. My eyes keep closing. Okay now, enough. I dab my chin, wipe my fingers. Ready to work. Ready now to come up with a *DOCTRINE*.

I settle myself back on the couch, one *DOCTRINE* coming right up. Sip from the goblet, but then—I can't help it—bound back up to lap down every meaty rosette left on the big slick platter. And then *what does it matter?* I am furiously slurping a final sublime bowlful of pears when the bellhop knocks again.

Throwing a couple of linen napkins over the licked-clean plates, I open the door to a second cart bearing multiple bottles of aquavit and dozens of little glasses. This time Carlos glides out from the bedroom, exclaiming, "Ah yes. Thank you." He signs the tab, saying, "That'll be all." Carlos (in actuality, I) must be spending three thousand dollars a day!

"An aquavit tasting," he says, "lingonberry, cucumber, ginger, lemongrass, pepper, and saffron. Hope you saved room."

Groaning, I plop back on the couch and say what I've been saying endlessly: "I can't do this."

Carlos kisses my flushed face. "Yes you can." I shake him off. (That little drama is wearing thin.) Then he's back on the phone and Maggie rolls her eyes and sits down. She says, "Too weird," and pouring us each a sample, "I've never had the saffron, have you?"

And, when I've got this and a linen napkin arranged on my lap, she passes me a glass of aquavit.

Which I haven't tasted before. And which, it turns out—with one sip—creates and fulfills and then recreates in me a craving of cartoonish intensity. That business with the meat and fruit, the chocolate truffles, the boat of vanilla-ginger sauce was nothing. A fleeting sensual moment brought on by my first real food in weeks. *Nothing like this!* This is beautiful! Sacred! Sublime! One sip of aquavit and all discomfort, every ill or hurt fades into nothing. It's impossible to describe. Except to say that flutes play and alleluia choruses resound. It's impossible to describe because the aquavit constitutes a realm where one's purpose in life appears clear, happy, and absolute. A realm where each glorious glassful sets my candy-red heart beating *big, bigger, biggest,* up out of my chest, where it sprouts wings and carries me off. ≈

Revelation

If everything happens for a reason,
If I can believe my own mind and heart,
If GOD comes when and where you least expect HIM,
THEN MAYBE I TRULY AM ON THE BRINK OF A
DIVINE LEAP.

Otherwise, what happened would probably count as a
garden-variety panic attack. I came to the Art Institute to get
out of the wind. I came to be among other real-life people with
real-life lives; and for the museum's pigment-preserving lighting, which seems so much more natural than the transient light
outside. I came because if I remained outdoors by myself
another minute, the sky and lake, the blistering wind, cars
racing past—all of it might dissolve at any second.

Here the hushed echoes from stately wing to stately wing,
the parade of sculptures and august paintings in the philan-
thropic air, offer calculated, temporary peace. A time outside
of time, with uniformed guards in every hall.

After Maggie's and my third or fourth glass of aquavit, we

discovered each glass was actually subtler (more *evocative* was the word we kept using) than the last. We kept toasting: "To this moment and that moment." "To right now." "To right *now.*" Carlos kept butting in his gray head, to ask, Did we mind? He was on the phone!

Maggie and I twined our arms, giggling and spilling. The main problem with a DOCTRINE, I told her, was that it was just so—so doctrinaire. "Why do we need it? Why do we need any of this? Isn't the whole thing 'Religion Without Rules?' So why am I supposed to invent a catechism here?"

I was standing a few inches from the glass wall, staring down at a line of cars snaking around the lake. Shafts of blue pierced through the clouds. An ache rose from my chest.

A voice, not as in "Do these voices command you to do things?" not, you know, a schizoid voice, more like the voice you hear when you hit the brakes a split second before a little child runs in front of your car—a warning voice filled the air. I stared down at Lake Shore Drive and spun in the room surrounded by sky as the warning voice said:

> *Colin and I stumbled on to the roof. We spun in each other's arms, reached for the stars and the moon. We spun and spun...*

Of course, this is what I tell myself whenever I recall what happened. *We spun and spun*—those are the words that come; that's as far as I go. What's strange is that this time the words occurred outside me. I heard them and didn't choke. They came on their own. Aloft in drunken fulfillment, my enormous magical winged heart leading the way, I lost my thrust, and a fluttery disquiet took hold. I flapped suspended, caught in an air pocket as a swift shadow of Colin flitted past.

"Whoa, Malcolm!" Maggie called. "Come and sit down." I was huffing and puffing and she said, "Shush. It's okay." She patted my shoulder and tried to reassure me with a string of gentle little jokes. But my lungs would not inflate completely. To my left, just out of sight, came a soft thud, perhaps a bird flying into the windowpane.

I jumped up and looked around, bristling with fear. What happened?

A leaf in a potted eucalyptus tree had sprung abominably to life—a praying mantis brushing against my ear, lighting on my cheek. Maggie jumped up, swept the leaf under the couch, and grabbed my hands. "More, more," she said. "What we need is more of this fabulous elixir." So we waded through the light pooling through the glass onto the lush carpet. We were clinking our dainty, brimming drinks, and smacking our lips.

And Maggie, her voice uncanny, said, "Do you *mind* keeping it down?" Tilting her head exactly like Carlos, wagging her finger, she said, "I *happen* to be on the phone."

Refilling our glasses, she raised hers up, and mimicked him perfectly: "The demon isn't as important as the struggle."

This got us giggling so that Carlos opened the door and matched her exasperated syllable for syllable. "Do you *mind* keeping it down? I *happen* to be on the phone."

Maggie and I were weeping, it was so funny. Carlos shook his head, and retreated to the bedroom. Maggie elbowed me and said, "Come on, Malkie. You try."

So I offered, "Loneliness is something to be achieved."

"Um? Try again."

"'What you don't *realize*, is that loneliness is something to be *achieved.*' I can't do him like you," I said and then, "*Oh*—" a surge from my poor overstuffed gut sent me stumbling into the mirror-paneled bathroom. After a couple of long, fast, relatively pain-free jets, I stared in the mirrors at an infinity of sweaty, over-indulged selves until I lost focus. Several unaccountable minutes later I emerged with a Sarah Vaughan song —something, something, *I love you so*—running through my head.

Maggie was in the bedroom with Carlos, who was shouting, "What were you thinking? He has to go on in a few hours!"

The incredibly sweet Sarah Vaughan lilted "...*strains of a mellow cello, when lights are low...*" as I downed cucumber aquavit straight from the bottle.

"You were just supposed to get him to eat and drink enough to calm down, enough to give him ballast for tonight's meeting."

"You should hear yourself!" Maggie said. "It's like he's the pet poodle and I'm the hired dog groomer!"

"No! *You* should hear *yourself*," Carlos yelled. "What does it say when you two get falling down, puke-in-your-soup drunk?"

Twirling through the room "...*soft and tender, love's all aglow...*" I raised my arms and puffed out my chest.

"Maggie, we have a group of very important, very busy, *wealthy* people coming tonight! *Not* the time to screw up!"

Standing close to the glass, I could hear the wind kicking and stalling. I stared down at the lake, which swelled and swooshed with white caps. The motion repeated in me—swelling and swooshing. I wanted a taste of fresh air, a walk outside, no, better yet, a flat-out, lung-burning run headlong into the wind.

"Seriously," Maggie slurred the word. "Spiff him up. Pouf up his tail, put a bow on his head…"

Pressed against the glass wall, I watched hundreds of people marching across the street. Veins of traffic stopped and started. Carlos and Maggie's voices rose and fell. But guess what? I got out: Elevator to the ground and through the revolving door. From one realm to another, I thought: This is just a test.

And then—smack into the stifling wind, I clapped my arms up near my head for protection. A man in a cape and top hat yelled through his cupped hands. He curled and uncurled his arm like a servile magician. He blew a big brass whistle and I shielded my eyes, staring up at the roof.

We spun in each other's arms. We reached for the stars and moon. We spun and spun and—and WE LET GO.
I spun to one edge. Colin spun to the other. Except he spun too far. Oh God, I can't stand this.
HE SPUN TOO FAR!

A geyser of hurt…

We spun playing statue maker on the roof.
We spun and let go.
I spun to one edge.
He spun OFF *the edge.*
My Fault Or His?

My fault or his? The words split me apart.

I had stepped into a blast-oven wind tunnel. The Swiss Crown hotel curves around a corner of Lake Shore Drive like an immense arc. I stared up at the building rising thousands of feet into the volcanic wind, and grasped the unreality of the sky and lake. Lovers embracing on the bridge, a dog on a leash, the grit in my teeth—everything, everything a trick of sound and light. Time was finally, finally going to tell. I couldn't sustain the illusion another second.

We held hands and let go. Staring straight into the sky, I anticipated a peeling away of everything, including myself. The scene was about to tear, and through the crack, a jagged line of truth would show. But just before the rip of something *real* through the sheet, a taxi appeared. A small but ordinary woman in a scarf dotted with sailboat insignias hobbled out in high heels. The doorman bowed and tipped his hat. (How did he manage to keep that hat on in this wind?) With a flourish, he opened a side door for her so she needn't propel herself through the revolving panels of glass and steel. And I turned away and broke down. She had no idea what she was in for. She, the doorman, me—none of us could grasp what we lost with every passing minute.

He spun off the edge. The taxi drove away, and the doorman popped back into his niche, leaving me bereft. I tucked my head and marched south, toward the museum.

I got sick again, in the gutter, anonymous traffic speeding past. Wiping my wretched mouth, I staggered up, blinking away tears. Children in a red car pointed at me and laughed. I must have looked comical, hands covering my face against the fumes, the lie, the accusation that had sent me running:

WHY'D YOU STOP, MALCOLM? WHY'D YOU STOP?

Overcome, I clenched my fists trying to rip through the sheet, and whispered fiercely, "Stop what? Stop you?"
STOP YOURSELF. ≈

Swiss Crown Suites 3601-3602, 3605-3607, 3609-3612 (week 10)

July 31

Dear Diary, Sorry I haven't written in ten days but I've been so-o-o busy building a religious empire! What with a round robin of RWR meetings and special fundraisers, and endless strategy sessions in our très elégante suites, I just haven't had the time or privacy, or frankly, the nerve, to pour my heart out.

After my little breakdown—in with the food and drink: out with the vomit, mucus, and tears—Carlos has hired a ghost writer for the DOCTRINE. Justin Eagan is an ex-Jesuit who writes spiritual news-letters. The DOCTRINE by yours truly will supposedly open doors for him. That's what Maggie and Carlos told him. "No, your name won't be on it, but rest assured: Time Will Tell, the World Will Know."

Small and fox-faced, Justin Eagan has oily, honey-colored hair, and a believable laugh. Going over the transcripts with him, Maggie finds endless excuses for squeezing his arm, patting his back, and "just forgive me a second," brushing up, and around him.

And: We've hired Tim and Janice, a sweet, humble brother and sister team, to videotape the meetings. Which, no need to tell you, Diary dear, are infomercials.

*

But okay, there's no need to feel *constantly* ashamed! Sometimes I go on stage and something mystical happens. Sometimes it's embarrassing and pathetic; sometimes it's magnificent. I stand in the wings, toss my hair, lick my lips, and bounce up and down. The lights dim, the crowd goes silent and I hurtle through space, landing deftly in the spotlight, arms outstretched, the better to embrace the first of the evening's many delirious ovations. I open my mouth and say stuff like: *"It doesn't matter what we think, we have to act." "If it's not impossible, why bother?" "If it is impossible, why try?"*

Carlos is right: it's easy. I say whatever pops to mind—I walk, talk, cha-cha-cha. Sometimes I hum a little and my words become a chant, my convictions a mantra.

Christ, how pretentious: Me and my mantra. Suffice it to say that I gesture, rave, whisper and pause, and everyone screams. Everyone leaps in ecstasy (or so it seems).

And—this is not good—lately I have to concentrate to keep from stroking myself! Adulation rushes in, enlarging me three or four times my normal size. My eyes start to roll and wings of exultation beat—THIS IS MY BODY, THIS IS MY BLOOD!

(Dear God, You have to forgive me! I did not ask for this.)

I did not ask for this but I'm at the point where even the money is starting to mean something to me. Stacks and stacks of it! More than any of us can count, when you factor in the electronic transfer, which is where Carlos says the real money comes in. Any time I think of it, I wonder: Am I essentially worth more than everyone else? I didn't used to be like this. But it takes real restraint not to preen. ≈

Thunder, Lightning Time

August 5

Yesterday, my parents phoned on their way to London. It took my father twenty minutes to track me down—why was I staying at the Swiss Crown? He preferred the Drake. My mother wanted to know where I'd be playing the second week of August. Wouldn't it be fun if they popped in for a meeting? "Name a day," I said. "I'll save you the best seats in the house." Immediately I almost threw up—*the best seats in the house*. Where did I think I was playing? Carnegie Hall? But they said they'd rather surprise me, sneak in, in the back when I wasn't expecting them. "We wouldn't want to throw you off your stride," my father said.

Then my mother grabbed the phone. "Oh Malcolm, I always knew you had a saintly aura about you."

So you can see, can't you, Diary Dear, why it might take an extra bit of gall to write you? And I've haven't even touched on the clairvoyant factor. Ensconced here in the suite with nothing to do but obey my insane captors, Carlos and Maggie, I find myself anticipating every antic act occurring within my sphere.

As I hung up, aghast at my chat with Mom and Dad, a picture flashed to mind: Carlos telling his computer: "Make a note to interview the parents. Get 'em on tape. Get 'em to sign a waiver."

Two seconds later, Carlos in the flesh says guess what, verbatim?!

If I didn't know better (and honestly, Dear Diary, I still *do* know better) I'd think the string of real-life events had gotten snarled up with my messiest, most nightmarish imaginings. In my head, Carlos makes a note, and immediately in real life puts it in writing: asterisk, word, exclamation point. A few weeks from now—I *know*—good old Mom and Pop will turn up on a talk show. I can hear them now:

Mother: "He was the most compassionate child. Even as a baby he had fits of empathy any time he saw a homeless person."

Father: "Malcolm is my only son. And as much as he mystifies me, I have to respect his new direction."

If only I didn't see these coincidences mounting. If only everyone and everything around me were not growing ever more predictable.

But then: oh wait a minute—I get it! You're downloading this! Aren't you, Carlos? What an idiot I am!

No wonder you're privy to my thoughts! I was stupid enough to think you were reading my mind, when actually, it's so obvious! You're reading my journal!

So okay. That being the case: Pay attention! This next thing I really want you to get, Carlos! Let this be your mantra, and maybe we can still avoid the cataclysm toward which we're obviously careening:

KEEP MY PARENTS OUT OF THIS!

Don't bother to argue, *my pet, my lover, tormentor, baby, honey, muffin,* because I know what you'll say. Believe me: my worry here has nothing to do with my own embarrassment (which via your plan, really does grow huger and more unsustainable by the minute) and everything to do with right and wrong. Really. It would be *wrong* to suck my parents into Religion Without Rules. They are a hundred times more naive than me.

So for all intents and purposes, Carlos, let's say my parents don't exist. Leave them out of this or I'll make you sorry. Thunder, lightning time: I've seen the light. You do what I say, Carlos! Or else I'll ruin you. Care to count the ways? ≈

Helpless But Not Innocent

August 6

Excuse me, Dear Diary, for getting so flagrantly sidetracked yesterday. Seventy-one days inside this fish tank with Carlos and Maggie! No wonder I am losing my mind.

Despite what I said before about Carlos tapping into my computer (which Maggie says is nuts: Carlos doesn't have time, and more, he just really doesn't care), this situation does foster an uncanny anticipation of one another's impulses. We know what's going to happen next because we're stuck in our adopted roles: my totally bored, totally frustrated inactivity when not on stage, Maggie as trusty baby-sitter, Carlos as nonstop Mr. Inside wheeler-dealer. We run through our miserable paces, think our guessable thoughts, and try not to notice the abyss widening beneath our feet.

We spun and spun!

My fault or his?

I did nothing! There's no going back, no way to will what happened not to have happened. I am stuck for all time, helpless but not innocent. ≈

Swiss Crown Suites 3301-3302, 3304-3305 (Week 11)

The thing that keeps me going is: The boy will come back. At every meeting now I peer out at the audience, clench my fists, close my eyes, and pray: please, please, appear. I jump from the dais, and on pretense of selecting someone to talk about "life as we know it," search every face. I grind my teeth and rub my eyes: Nothing, and no one.

And yet, a tightness in my neck, a throbbing red line around my field of vision, a jigsaw in my head. A harsh cry goes forth and the Great Prophet knows: His Truly Beloved Will Return to Him In a New Manifestation.

This Manifestation may lurk in shadows, waiting for a lull. But it's so close; I can feel it. The boy's young, just-woken-up-after-working-all-day scent, his lithe, just-stretching air, the tantalizing glint and sheen of his eyes and hair hover on the periphery of everything I think and do.

When I'm not acting as Millennial Prophet for Religion Without Rules, I wander the streets, doggedly tracing my tracks. Tyler appeared luminously before me, and the moment

I tried to put myself near him—I am just like you!—he vanished. I no sooner found the *soul of concern, of sweetness, light, peace, joy and hope* than I lost him.

So now, acting on faith, I float aimlessly, deliberately unawares. I am not hunting him. Because you don't set out to snare the soul of concern, of sweetness, light, et cetera. You respect his freedom. You calmly accept his absence and wait in joyful hope that he will return to you. ≈

It Won't Be Long

I wish. I solemnly, desperately wish it were enough that he exists. But it's gotten to the point where, when I'm not performing, I lock myself in one of the four mirrored bathrooms. (We moved to the 33rd floor yesterday. Now we're back in two double suites. One is devoted to junk from Maggie's shopping sprees and the devotees' endless offerings. Devotees? I mean "fans." Their gifts include everything from valuable antiques to weird little packets of feathers and dust. Once we received a live turtle hidden in a fake book, and once a baby ferret in a Bloomingdale's box. Maggie arranged for Elise Salmonschneider, an earnest, animal-loving friend of Stephanie's, to take them to a shelter on Foster Avenue.) Anyway. Two or three times a day a kind of break develops, and having learned from experience, I race to the bathroom before the shifting universe exposes boundless injury and injustice. And what do I do? I just hold on. Lost in the infinite mirrored walls, I brace myself between tub and sink. Blood roaring in my ears, sorrow clawing my spine, I hold on with all my might.

I'm down to 175 pounds, just five more than I weighed the day Colin died. Yesterday Maggie took me out to buy an interactive scale—you can turn off the monitoring voice, thank God—and a rowing machine the cost of which could feed a family for a week, despite the fact that the hotel's gym is as big as any in the city, with a swimming pool and spa, which, it's true, I'm not comfortable using. Also several upgrades to the hotel's entertainment system, ours to keep, of course. So, great —you'd think I'd be happy.

But the only reason I leave my holding pattern between the tub and sink is: The boy might come back. The phone might ring; the concierge has a message: Tyler is waiting in the lobby. He's slinking behind a potted palm. He's sitting next to a marble column, rattling a newspaper, and dabbing at the scant mustache he's too young, really, to grow. Or—in a mall, we pass each other on crisscrossing escalators. We nod, unable to keep from smiling, because we both know: It won't be long. Soon we'll be together forever. Nothing on earth is more inevitable.

Then, next fantasy, he stops at one of the bakeries where I go to bless the bread. I spend extra time on the dough, slapping and punching it before moving on to the éclair ceremony. After drizzling chocolate on dozens of trays, I slowly eat a big one filled with chocolate custard between layers of double-chocolate fondant. My hands are sticky with frosting, slick with custard, and as I daintily wipe them clean, there in front of me are his hands, pressed together for me to kiss. I whisk off my apron and sash, and off we go, the boy Tyler and I, west on Erie Street, holding sticky hands. With each passing block, State Street, Dearborn, LaSalle, Halsted, I grow younger and younger, while Tyler melds with, and generates, his twin. By Sheffield, Tyler and Colin and I are jumping from rooftop to rooftop, shooting water pistols and yelling:

WHY'D YOU DO IT?
DO WHAT?
WHY'D YOU JUMP?
FOR FUN, YOU FREAK.
HEY, WHADDA YOU KNOW?
IT
DOESN'T
HURT
A
BIT.
≈

By My Fingertips

When, when, when? When can I go home? I don't care if the shop's done! I'll camp out in a sleeping bag on the terrace if I have to. Okay? But I can't stand the Swiss Crown another hour. It's not real, it's horrible, it's nothing but interim. I mean: What am I doing here? Besides standing stupefied as my frantic musings take shape, flap and splat.

So I'm going to tell Carlos: "I am going home this minute, to my one true shop whether completely transmogrified or not."

But when I peer in at him, he's sitting before two computer screens, sweating so profusely it's dripping on the keyboard. He's swiveling in his chair, rubbing his face, and whispering, "fuck, fuck, fuck!"

Even though he's freshly shaven and dressed like a billionaire, I see a hard-core gambling addict hitting bottom. "Anything wrong?" I ask. "I know the market plummeted yesterday."

"And the day before," Carlos says. "Really, it's been shit all week. And last. But not to worry. These fluctuations are factored into our timetable."

"Oh, I'm sure," I say, and try to not to smile, an expression he misreads. For, were Religion Without Rules to collapse, I could reclaim my life. I could stop endlessly rationalizing. Stop swallowing the guilt and sorrow surging forth every time someone wants me to heal them, to strengthen and enrich them, make their mother sane, their brother walk, their boy- or girlfriend love them again. Were this all to unravel, I could get back to selling baked goods, pouring coffee; and at the end of every day, simply, honestly, cashing out.

"No, seriously," Carlos tries to reassure me. "Everything's going to be fine. The Linden Street shop is done. We're moving back Sunday afternoon."

I gasp and turn my head, tears springing to my eyes. My wish so strong, that I can't deny or disguise it, even if this is Carlos. Even if I should know better. "Don't tease me about this, Carlos."

"I'm not," he says.

"Sunday afternoon," I say.

"That's right," Carlos says, his air of panic gone.

I grip my hands together to keep them from shaking. And that other part of me, which hardly ever speaks, pipes up: Just relax, Malcolm. No one scores a hundred. And this is it—the reason you're alive. ≈

Sammy's All Nite (1)

Early this evening, after a meeting in the Equitable Building, Carlos dispatched the throng in the lobby, saying, "If you want to join the acolytes, call the number on your program." Arms high, palms pushing forward, he steered the crowd into the rain. The RWR intimates, Stephanie and Rafe, Louie, Demetria, Lyle, Elise Salmonschneider, *et al.*, Carlos sent on various last-minute, late-night missions. Or maybe he sent them to the movies, I don't know. He got rid of them somehow, real fast.

Yet it didn't occur to me that Carlos might have gotten rid of Maggie, too, until we stepped into the elevator. As the automatic doors closed, I realized Carlos and I had not been alone together, without Maggie, for more than a month. Fingertips tingling, I stared at my shoes, and asked, "Where is she?"

"Who, your mommy?"

"My dog groomer."

"Spending the night with a couple of friends, Sarah and

Tara or the other two, Rena and Nina. They all come to the meetings, and they all look alike."

At the car, I dug through my vestments for the key. Carlos stepped almost on top of me. "You're going to drive?"

"It's my car."

"Oh, well," Carlos said, "by all means then."

But I simply could not find my keys, and Carlos, who was still standing almost on top of me, sighed and shifted his weight. He rolled his eyes and whistled in his patented, sarcastic way of "Hey, I have all day here."

Clammy with anger and (though I'm loathe to admit it) a tinge of fear, I tore off the pink cummerbund. Carlos then tossed a ring of keys in the air and speared it with his index finger. "If you will…" he said, "…allow me." He opened the driver's door with a flourish, and motioned me around to the passenger's side.

Whereupon, I almost ran off. I saw myself charging through the parking garage, and it was the echo, I think, that kept me rooted to the spot. The echo of my footsteps resounding through the underground parking lot would be utterly ridiculous, and Carlos knew it.

So I got into the car. We were only four blocks from the Swiss Crown. The rain made the windows fog up and the defroster didn't work. Carlos smeared the condensation with the back of his hand. "In five weeks we'll have our custom Mercedes."

I didn't say, "A Buick Le Sabre not only restores your faith, it rejuvenates your soul." Or, "If all the people in the country came together to share their hopes and dreams and what they wanted most in the world, you might end up with the BMW X6."

I merely said, "Ah yes, the Tao of the Sacred Luxury Automobile."

"Damn right," he said. "This is nothing if not a red-blooded, God-fearing, capitalist religion."

In the hotel's garage, he rapped on the bullet-proof window and whistled in the elevator. "Come on, come on," he said holding the doors for me.

Inside our adjoining suites, the stage was set: diaphanous curtains drawn, champagne on ice, lights low. Here I should have run. But for some reason I wavered.

"Um, just remembered something—I'll be back later," I thought of saying.

Or, "Pretty tired, guess I'll catch some z's."

Of course, why I wasted even a second contemplating these stupid gambits is a mystery. Why I didn't heed the instinct coursing through every cell of my being to get out of there is beyond my paltry reasoning. A case of total system failure: I stood there like an idiot as Carlos sat on the huge white couch and patted the spot next to him.

"How can you stand this?" I asked.

And Carlos stretched out his legs, propping his feet on the coffee table. "Relax," he grinned, laying his arm on the top of the couch. "Pigeon. Baby. Muffin."

The heat flickering off my face subsided enough for me to fake a laugh, "Ha-ha," pace the length of the room, and circle back. "Everything you're doing, Carlos, is, like, straight out of Uncle Billy's Big Book of Sleaze."

"Come on, Malcolm. We're celebrating our last night here. Linden Street's beautiful. We'll be back before dinner tomorrow."

The promise of Linden Street—home tomorrow!—sent another heat, this time internal, fanning from my stomach through my chest. Alight, aglow, I managed to speak in a hoarse, bemused croak: "Excuse me, Carlos, but—." A silvery bolt flashed in front of my eyes. "Before dinner tomorrow? You're sure?"

Carlos said, "We'll be ensconced before tea," and once again my lungs filled with excess air, sweeping me up off my feet, so that I drifted, settling gently beside him on the couch. My backside stuck to the leather upholstery. I shifted my weight and the cushions squeaked. The space between Carlos and me took on a palpable charge. And then, you had to be there, I am not exaggerating: a hush fell; all the car alarms for miles around went silent and the maids outside our door sang a lilting roundelay up and down the carpeted corridor.

Carlos stroked my head with his long-fingered hand, and despite myself, I leaned into him, pressing my ear to his heart. He clicked on the giant-screen TV and—the lion lay down with the lamb; the seas parted: There I was, purring and panting at Carlos's touch as strobe-action videos washed over us.

After a minute, though, a flash of survival crackled through. I started to get up but Carlos yanked me back down by the elbow. My other elbow swung around and smashed him in the face. I said I was sorry. It was an accident. "I know it was," he said, crumpled with apparent pain. And you'd think I'd know better, but on reflex I bent down to see where he hurt. Whereupon, Carlos lunged forth, swinging me in a choke hold. His leathery face rubbed mine with citrus and resin. His bristly, shorn head passed under my chin. I couldn't sit up. Face to face, he grabbed my ears and used his thumbs to stretch the skin at my temples. His tongue tasted cool and dry, but after a second I remembered my priorities and bit down. He pressed his thumbs against my windpipe. I tried to heave him up, off of me, when the glass coffee table went over. The champagne and ice bucket crashed against the metal legs. I twisted loose but he grabbed me and pulled me down. Kneeling on my kidneys, Carlos tore at my clothes, buttons popping from my shirt, seams of my pants ripping. I screamed "Carlos stop!" and—surprisingly—he did. We both moaned and rolled apart on the floor.

And still I could have left, but didn't. Carlos was gasping and grinning, and the fingers of his right hand rested lightly on my collarbone. Had I jerked away and jumped up, he would have let me go. Had I thrown on some clothes and rushed out to Sammy's (where I am right now), Carlos would not have pursued me. I'm sure. His wonderfully skillful hand would have come up in a salute, like "All right, chief, see ya later," and that would have been that.

But. I picked up chips of ice from the carpet and rubbed them into nothing on my belly. My eyelids fluttered and I leaned back, sitting on my heels. I said, "Okay," and I arched forward, right under his nose, "Okay, Carlos, okay."

And once we started, we were at it for hours. A rising hum lapped at the walls. A pair of mischievous, winged sopranos flitted among the cathode rays. This time, returning to our original positions, I was the man on top and he was the man who screamed.

And afterwards Carlos was the one who lay too gaga to move. His mouth gaped, his eyes rolled back. Newly fortified, hyper awake, I showered and shaved while Carlos slipped from a daze into sleep. I dressed in soft new clothes (courtesy of Maggie's shopping compulsion), and then I lifted Carlos tenderly off the floor, and carried him, skinny, brown, floppy with sleep, to the enormous, tightly made bed. I tucked him in and went out for a bite. ≈

Sammy's All Nite (2)

August 18

At Sammy's, I ate a bacon cheeseburger and drank a few beers. I lingered over my notebook as the bartender conspired with a lively gray haired woman drinking Drambuie and holding a fluffy white kitten in her arms. The only other customers were two couples sporting drastic face piercings. As I packed up my notebook and laid down my money, all six people converged on me. "You're him," said a girl with shimmering aqua hair.

"Who?"

"You know," said a man, a spike through his nose.

"The guy."

They asked for my autograph. I signed a bunch of cocktail napkins and shook their hands. The bartender set my dishes on a shelf as if for display but the gray haired woman waved for him to take them back down. As I left, they were dabbing their fingers in my leftover ketchup-smeared grease.

And—it didn't bother me!

I walked away amazed. This whole night the scales did not fall from my eyes so much as gradually dissolve. I mean, really, what's the big deal? I prance on stage telling everyone I do not have the answers; we ask the wrong questions, because we're compelled to ask the wrong questions; it's human nature. The feeling comes and goes, but I walked out of Sammy's with the dawning of a realization. RWR is nothing new!

Nothing I say or do is. But if a few people think I give them hope, well, maybe I do. Maybe I'm laying the foundation. Because everyone should ask for faith: Not for a heartbeat should anyone take anything for granted.

At four a.m., I sauntered out of the bar where a lifetime ago Colin and I drank vodka Collinses. And I was less weary, less frightened than I can ever remember being. Sated with food and drink, I headed toward Lake Michigan to watch the sun rise. I walked for miles along the shore, balancing on huge, jagged rocks as waves splashed over my sneakers. I teetered and slid, arms open to the wind. If people want to give me money, why should I subject myself to misery in response? If Carlos and his high-stakes portfolio bring in more money, more bakeries, more infomercials, why not enjoy the ride? You could even make the case that I'm obligated to enjoy it. Just as you could argue the semi-opposite—that I must alleviate a cubic foot of someone's personal anguish for every dollar we accept. Either way. Whatever comes. One is just as impossible as the other. In the grainy shadows of gray before daybreak, I walked along the rocks in rhythm, *step* as the relentless waves pulled, *land* as they hit. My legs and feet were numb; the rest of me rose up. The waves pounded all around me, and I lifted my arms, tilted my face, held my breath—hoping, aching—for what? The boy Tyler? Colin? The chance to go back and undo my worst mistakes? The waves crashed and churned. The magic words, the lost prayer, the boys' promises sprayed up from the lake.

Eventually the sun came up in a dirty sky. I trudged along Lake Shore Drive toward the Loop. A sidewalk vendor sold me a pair of Chinese slippers. I trashed my soggy Cons, walked four more blocks, then crouched on the Art Institute steps until it opened.

*

After looking at all the famous paintings—A giant pink mother and her chunky baby; women bathing behind a bank of ferns; a bowl of pears; a crucifixion in the abstract—I sat on the banquette outside the cafeteria with another man who also wrote in a notebook. Old ladies on their way to English muffins and tea argued about an exhibit of Holocaust sculptures. The man on the bench with me, like the clientele at Sammy's, wore theatrical make-up. Glittery waves of green rose up from his eyelids. His big loose mouth was hi-lighter pink and greasy-looking.

*

Exhausted, oddly redeemed and chastened, I thought of returning to the hotel but realized that Carlos and Maggie would probably have checked out by now. They had probably moved to Linden Street already. So I decided to go there.

*

Only guess what: We didn't move. The shop was not ready. Carlos lied. He had told me what I wanted to hear so he could have his way with me. Surprise, surprise. "*Oh no*," Carlos said, shocked—*shocked*. "The workmen exaggerated, that's all." ≈

PART THREE: Failure Makes You
             More of Who You Are

Fear Enters, Stage Left

"Tick tock," Maggie says. Wearing chiffon pants and a goofy green hat, she taps her feet and raps her knuckles. "What's with you," she asks, "why can't you hurry?" She's swatting her leg, waving me through. "Good-bye hotel room, good-bye view." The door slams behind us. "Jesus. Man. At last."

So finally. *Today's the day!* For real. Linden Street's finished. Carlos has been there since dawn, waiting to give us the grand tour.

And even before we're out of the building, I can tell this afternoon is one of those days when everything seems too saturated with color and grace. Silken breezes flit through the station wagon's open windows. Gentle, tree-filtered light imbues the world with a shimmering glow. Tooling along Lake Shore Drive, I am foreign, even extraneous, to this paradise. Blue blue *blue* sky and a patchwork of green, marked by red-and gold-edged leaves that flutter in the air. The outside world seems too real to be real. Everything outside the car—outside of me—is more pulsatingly *alive* than I could ever be.

I feel like saying, "*God!* All right, already, I give up! I admit You exist! Now can You please *ease up?* Turn the intensity down a notch before it kills me."

Without thinking I say to Maggie, "Earthly beauty is so…

"What?" She turns down the music, but I shake my head, and turn it back up. It's too hard to say out loud.

The earthly beauty is staggering. The day, the world, the whole set-up is unbelievably gorgeous. I wouldn't trade this afternoon for anything. Except, well…a little dazzling beauty goes a long way. I get lost in the vastness pretty fast. Within minutes every glimmer, every soft-focused transformation lodges a painful, blinking pressure behind my eyes. The swirl and throb of the scenes unfolding bring on a shudder that turns to a sob. It's too much and not enough!

For one minute the world is cold and empty, bereft of meaning. God is Nowhere and Nothing, a Necessary Fiction to keep any half-rational species from killing itself. And the next —in the next moment the merest particle of dust in a sunbeam, a branch in the wind, puddle on the pavement are microcosms of God's…what? Love, I guess, is the word. Why is it the flimsiest Manifestation-Of-Something-I-*Might*-Be-Able-To-Believe-In tears me apart? Sunshine, hydrangeas, and back-lit, just-turning copper beeches feel like the heel of a boot on my neck. Songs on the radio, Maggie's patter, we're almost home—blood in my mouth, gasoline in my eyes. And yet also —ecstatic bliss! Terrible, terrible joy! I just don't know how to express it.

I don't know what to *do* with it. Except to admit:

ALL RIGHT, ALL RIGHT, ALREADY, YOU EXIST! I BELIEVE!

I'm weeping and shaking and Maggie says maybe I better pull over. Patting my back, she says, "It's all right. Don't worry. The end of summer really gets to me too."

Sniffling, bobbing my head, I try to shake it off with, "Oh wow." And: "Maggie, I'm fine. It's nothing." I promise to maintain the rest of the way home. But—

Home! Home! Home! I want it so much my eyes fill, my arms ache! We're *so close!* I want it *so bad!* The scene through the windshield becomes a blur, and I can't breathe. To keep myself in one piece, I deliberately fantasize about sabotage. I concentrate on an urge to litter—to toss huge non-biodegradable banana peels in the path of all the other bright, sleek machines speeding along with us. Maggie tips her head, holding on to her hat. Her teeth shine. Her skin gleams. Another transforming occasion, another occurrence of Beauty and Light and I swear I'm going to die. I'm going to scream. How much are we supposed to take?

"Will you relax?" Maggie says.

And I say, "Relax? What a concept! *Relax, relax, relax!* Now why didn't *I* think of that?" Tears are streaming down my face.

"Hey, come on," Maggie says, "let me drive."

"No way," I say, "we're almost there!" *We're almost, almost home!* Signal, go left, through a few stop signs and...I see it! There it is! The facade is white stucco with brown trim. We park in front. Red and purple flowers cascade from window boxes on all three stories. Geraniums, mums, and marigolds flourish in huge stone planters flanking the door.

The shop inside is at least three times its former size. Four tables fit in the north window now, not two. Instead of a glass display case and Formica countertop, a mantle of burled wood curves through the room. The kitchen is immense, and immaculate.

Upstairs, six square dormitory rooms branch off a long hallway with bathrooms at both ends. Carlos, having kept a wary distance since our last little tryst, leads the way up another flight to my quarters, which include an enormous bathroom, a balcony facing east, and a sunlit space for study and meditation.

It's great. Just great. Windows everywhere, pale hardwood floors, wainscoting, skylights…I tell myself not to panic. There's an intimidating expanse of space. A cavernous echo. And that electrical, headachy smell of plaster and paint. "Nice," I say. "Cheery…" and start toward the designer bathroom where two plumbers are working.

Mr. Andersen, a somber, wiry black man, of Andersen Plumbing and his young assistant in a beret—*not,* my fingers tingle, my eyes shut, my hair prickles, *Tyler!*—are installing a whirlpool mechanism in the fits-four fake marble tub. I back away, inhale, exhale; squint, cock my head. And, okay, brave another glance at the young assistant. In passing, from a distance, he resembles Tyler just enough to sting me. And the beret: are all the hot young guys wearing them suddenly?

But I'm *fine.* This is great. And to prove it, here I go, on to my lovely new balcony. A grove of trees stretches below. I turn in a circle, thinking *pouf, take me back!* Please Maggie! Carlos!

Put everything back the way it used to be. I want my life that's vanished without a trace returned at once. I'm going to count to ten, snap my fingers, and then— I will see it's a joke. A sound stage for a TV show. "Today's Pious Lifestyles."

I mean, how can I be alive when no remnant of my previous life remains? Where are my books and pictures, my clothes and furniture? Where in the world has my modest but real existence *gone?*

Maggie at least gets what's happening, and tries to comfort me. With her arm over my shoulder, she whispers, "Don't worry, Malkie. Once we decorate it, give it some of your personal style, it's going to be great. Look..." She reaches into the pack swinging on her shoulder. "I've got some catalogs we can go through. Pottery Barn, Crate and Barrel..." Through clenched teeth she hisses at Carlos. "Why are you just standing there? Can't you get him a tranquilizer or something?"

"Uh no," I speak up. "I don't need a tranquilizer. All I need is a minute." I turn away, back from the balcony, and bow my head. I need a minute to convince myself that the room, the people, the babbling voices are real. I'm Malcolm Tully standing in my new room in my new shop the first Sunday in September. Everything makes sense, everything adheres to a clear-cut logic of cause and effect. So why am I wiping my eyes? Why do I suspect I've stood here forever, hopelessly trapped in a tangled-up ball of time?

"Hold up," I say, "I'm all right." And my words echo, the moment resounds: I've stood here and said this before. I've always stood here. The rest is a fairy tale—We're all of us trapped in the moment. My God! Why didn't we realize this sooner? We should pray. We should get down on our knees.

"Are you sure you're okay?" Carlos sounds genuinely concerned. Or no, more than concerned—*Carlos is scared!*

I take Maggie by the shoulders as if she'd never believe me otherwise, and say, "We should pray."

"Okay."

"No, I'm serious. I mean it."

"I mean it, too," she says. "We have a lot to be thankful for."

But I scoff at this. "I don't mean praying like *that*, like we're in nursery school."

"Oh."

"No, no, Maggie," I instantly repent. "I'm stupid and wrong and you're right. We're *supposed* to pray like we're in nursery school. We're supposed to be the Lord's little lost lambs."

Maggie shakes her head. "I think you were right the first time. It's important to use our whole minds."

"Absolutely," I say. "Absolutely, that's important, that's as important you can get!" I can hear myself shouting; but I can't stop. My voice embarrasses me but I'm sounding a battle cry: "What we need," I thunder, "what we *desperately* need is every bit of substance we can muster."

"Amen," Maggie says.

"Amen," Carlos says. He turns on his heel, computer-tablet under his arm, and points a finger at Maggie. "Don't let him out of your sight."

"You're going to get him some professional help," Maggie says, "Right away." ≈

Baby

You may not believe this. Or, I don't know, maybe you saw it coming all along. But I've turned into a gigantic baby. My mommy never leaves my side. She sleeps on the floor by my bed. She brings me glasses of water, reads to me, and combs my hair. And my daddy checks on me every few hours. "How's he doing? Has he been crying?" My Mommy Maggie and my Daddy Carlos hover over me and whisper anxiously in the corner. "Is he eating? Is he sleeping?" "How does he seem?" After dinner they dress me up and show me off. I toddle out on stage, chortling and waving my arms. In front of the video camera, I scream and stomp, jibber and jabber and everyone oohs and ahhs and says how adorable. ≈

Just Find the Boy

RWR pumps in great gushers of money, but we're more leveraged than Niagara Falls. When I ask about the bottom line, red or black, Carlos pats my hand. "Don't worry," Daddy says. "Let me keep the books."

"Gee, Carlos, let me keep a shred of autonomy."

"Go ahead." He swallows hard. "Keep one." I shift my gaze and catch a yellow patch of tension around his mouth, a darting shadow from his averted eyes. This past week I've picked up intimations, but now it's obvious: The Man, the Ringmaster, the Big, Big Daddy is very, very afraid. What if I quit? Disappear? Kill myself? Then what will he do?

I detest this *religioso* stuff. All I wanted was exactly what Maggie said we'd have if I didn't declare myself "Spiritual Leader." Remember? A coffee klatch with pretensions. That's what she said; that's what I wanted; and that's all! Except naturally, setting up my utter downfall, for about two minutes there, I also wanted to sit in the middle as Carlos circled the room, manipulating twin sets of iron balls in his hands. Two minutes, two weeks, it was a blip of desire. If only I could go back to that point—return to my old shop, the blizzard, Carlos's sheet of damp hair…

But wait. You know how if you act happy you sometimes almost feel happy? If he wanted to, Carlos could scrounge up my old robe in a minute; rotate the silvery chiming balls in his hands, and bound around me on his mesmerizing feet. (And you'd do it in a minute, wouldn't you, Carlos? You'll do whatever I say, whatever it takes.)

But I'm really not interested in your flapping robe anymore. What I want is simple. Nothing impossible; no going back in time. Just find Mad Mike and his crew. Set them up in some warehouse where I can go watch the old sots rev their saws and smoke their spliffs as the boy trips over to me in his overly big boots, blue jeans slipping from his hips. Hire them all to play it out, over and over: the beer-bellied crew belching and farting; the beautiful boy bowing to me, doffing his hat, spilling his gorgeous curls in front of my face; the gaggle of rough drunks spitting and swearing as the boy takes my hand, asking me, *do I mind?*

You still need me, Carlos. You may always need me! So, why not do this: Forget the drunks and warehouse. Just find the boy Tyler for me and give him my tidings.

Tell him who I am but don't coerce him. Just show him where I wait. And when *the soul of concern, of sweetness, light, peace, joy and hope* appears at my side, we will blow you kisses. We will wave to you from the balcony, Carlos, the beautiful boy and I, blowing you kisses and calling, "Ta-ta!" ≈

On Second Thought, Don't Find the Boy

All I ask is that Tyler come to me of his own accord. The way I see it: If my heart never wavers, if I devote myself to him entirely—no doubts or errant, ulterior motives—he will naturally, eventually, make his way to my arms.

But, but, but—I'm banging my head against the wall! Because my purest, most constant prayer—that someday he be drawn to me—is wrong. Praying that Tyler seek me is coercive in itself. I want him to want me, when it should be enough that he exists!

Just as: *it should be enough that Colin existed once.* We had six magical months together, and now after all these years, a miracle: A supernatural impression of Colin as the boy Tyler has appeared before me. My unexpected glimpse of that luminous face should sustain me the rest of my days. Except the moment I think the vision can—and will—I am lost. Once I am saved—I am *not* saved! It's as if: He lives on. And I am dead. ≈

Massive Portentous Fraudulence

September 21

The new shop is so graceful, stately, and tranquil as to suggest the antithesis of a shop. It hardly seems possible anything so crass as commerce, so gross as chewing and swallowing transpires here. Oh, people eat, but with such rapt concentration the act borders on prayer. They pay, but so wholeheartedly each transaction seems like a sacred offering. Semi-subliminal hymns fill the air but not constantly; every now and then the shuffle function selects a pause.

At the west entrance, long contemplative lines of seekers progress to the takeout counter. At the east entrance, people take off their shoes and make themselves ready for one of twenty-one pedestal tables, waited on by willowy girls in long dresses, their hair pulled into buns and wreathed with flowers. Sylvia's Korean; Annick is Dutch, and their ceremonial, sometimes faltering English adds to the portentousness.

Carlos in his fine suits and pristine Adidas oversees the operation with a sacerdotal air. He oversees the bakers, now called novitiates, who also wear white Adidas. (Do you suppose he's gotten a sponsorship deal?) Anyway: Carlos oversees the clerks who wear white or black clothes and brightly patterned vests, and either shave their heads or wear their hair in long glossy ponytails down their backs. Graham (tawny curling ponytail) works the main room with Sylvia and Annick. Greg (dark hairless head, blazing white smile) works the takeout counter, ringing up sales; while upstairs, four more handsome young clerks man the computers.

I, on the other hand, pad about with no honest work. Other than performing the nightly meeting, I hardly speak, because basically, I don't know what to say to people anymore. Everywhere I go, novitiates, clerks, acolytes, and customers are waiting to venerate me. Sometimes they bow their heads before casting a shy glance. Sometimes they freeze, open-mouthed. Or they stare and nudge each other. But invariably when I enter a room, they stop what they're doing. The bolder, more desperate ones vie for eye contact. Everyone looks at me expectantly, so, *so* expectantly, and I...

I stumble and blush, hurrying to the nearest exit, blush and lurch along as people reach for my hem, jostling each other, trying to grasp my hand. I blush and stammer, "Yes," and "Hello."

"Yes." "Hello." It's ridiculous.

Your little girl's dying of cancer? "Yes." I pat the mother's hand.

You lost your job? "Hello." I squeeze the man's shoulder.

AIDS? "Yes."

I crouch by his wheelchair and awkwardly try to hug him, "Hello."

Lied, cheated, stolen—third time in rehab? "Hello." I nod at the addict, "Yes—" admire his red suspenders.

What's that? You feel compelled to drive your car onto the tracks of a speeding train? "Hello." Play with a loaded gun? "Yes." Breathe carbon monoxide? "Well yes, have faith... hello."

I ought to be shot.

And yet everyone oohs and ahs about my aura, my chakras, my chi. I stammer and blush, utter inanities when I can bring myself to utter anything at all—and no one complains. No one raises a fist, tears at the curtains, nothing. Customers, clerks, acolytes, all, raise their eyes, clasp their hands, and proclaim that my very presence fills them with beatitude. ≈

I Peer Over the Edge

Tonight my biggest fear (now my ex-biggest fear) came true, and nothing happened. Slinking among the nether reaches of my mind, along with, "what if I die? what if I've *already* died and this murk of uncertainty, this frantic limbo of futility is my eternal punishment?" has lurked, till now, a more distinct fear: What if I walk on stage, open my mouth before a full house, and nothing comes out?

What if I just stand there, swaying?

Well, tonight, stone dumb, I closed my eyes and smoothed the vestment. The skirt swished like a tablecloth around my legs and I forgot where I was. Or no, that's not right. *I didn't care where I was!* The hundred-some heads expecting a trans-cendental balm for their suffering, or at least some answers from me, sputtered: What the hell was going on? Why weren't they getting what they came for?

Again I opened my mouth and closed it. A widening ripple of impatience fanned through the crowd. Mass indignation developed tooth and nail. The mood in the room took the form of an animal on the loose, snarling and rank, loping through the aisles. Instinctively, I tore off the fatuous toga-thing and stuffed it under the stage chair. But by the time I turned around, flexing my legs, ready to fend for my life, the first signs of riotous anger were already dwindling to a few listless harrumphs. The wild unstoppable beast vaporized before my eyes into mutterings—into mere rustlings in the back row.

Prompting me finally to find my voice, and yell: "Hey, come on! Don't do this!" I crouched in front of them, hands extended, screaming: "Rip into me, why don't you?"

I waited red-faced and huffing. I tried to reason with them: "What kind of messiah can I be if no mob of furious, tortured souls rises up to destroy me?"

Nothing. They just gazed at me as if in a trance and then—worse—the unthinkable—they folded their chairs and got down on their knees. They put their hands together and closed their eyes.

I even said, "What is this? Some kind of joke?"

But they didn't answer. They didn't budge.

"Get out of here," I yelled. "Go on! Go away!" I screamed: "Get the fuck out of here! Now!"

When would this end? Why didn't they leave?

And then it dawned on me—*I* could just go. Except if I headed for the front door, they might crush me from all sides. Hadn't I just commanded them to *rip into me*? So, I inched off the stage slowly, as slowly as if trying to sneak out of a lion's lair (the worshipful penitent animal being just as dangerous as the savage angry one). I backed off the stage, and opened the fire escape door.

An alarm sounded and several security guards came running, but I got away. I ran to the lake, the wind battering me from all directions. Sand stuck in my nostrils, under my eyelids, inside my mouth. My shop, my life, everything I do—have nothing to do with me anymore. ≈

A Cold Kernel of Evil

After last night, Carlos says they no longer need me at the meetings. Early this morning when he and Maggie convene in my chambers to review the daily agenda, he says, "Malcolm, now that we're in multimedia we can run things on auto-pilot."

"Great."

"You should only show up if you feel like it. From now on, let's say you make, oh I don't know, one appearance a week."

"Fine."

"At most."

"Fine."

"We don't want to overexpose you."

"Of course not," I say, still in my nightshirt. "Mercy me, anything but!" I breeze about the room. "Saints preserve us. Lord, deliver us. Anything, anything but overexposure!"

Carlos and Maggie exchange glances as I throw open the balcony doors and lean seductively over the railing. "Uh,

Malcolm?" Maggie waves to me from six feet away. "Are you sure you're all right?"

"Never better." I rub my hands together. "Now first off, my darlings, let me just say I agree with you totally: multi-media's the *only* way. Starting, I think, with music: we're going to need hymns, carols, requiems, maybe even—" I stare hard at Carlos, then Maggie, "rock videos." (Though no one has actually mentioned it to me, I know that Louie and Lyle have cut a CD based on—and named—"The Doctrine." And that, a music video of the title track features the famous gospel singer, Letitia Wright, who as luck would have it, happens to be Lyle's cousin's godmother.)

Hanging my butt over the railing, I say, "Every religion has its own music." But so coolly, so casually do Carlos and Maggie not react that I decide to throw back my head like a movie star and intone, "Music, music…" And shifting my weight—look Ma, no hands—scissor my legs. "Mu-oo-sic!" Maggie gasps and Carlos lunges to save me. His long, hot hands fly to my sides. Half a heartbeat more and he'd have scooped me forcibly inside. Instead, rage and embarrassment at succumbing to my little trick ripple across his face, withering it to a leathery pouch.

He recoups with a meditative hand to his chin. "Actually," he says, "we're investing quite a bit in a CD *and* a DVD."

"Really?" And mea culpa; I cannot, to save my life, resist the stance of Holy Man here. Feet apart, arms raised to embrace the sky, I adopt an expression of divine inspiration. It's as simple as posing for a photograph. You lift your arms, tilt your head to heaven, and imagine pure white rays of rapture flowing through your glorified body.

"From this time forward," I hum, I chant, flashing my teeth at the sun, "let there be *music* at the meetings." I wave my arms and smile at Maggie and Carlos in all innocence. "What do you think? Can we," I revert to a more regular voice and posture, "get Louie and Lyle to play for us?"

"Why couldn't we get them?" Carlos counters.

"Aren't they awfully big-time all of the sudden?"

"Louie and Lyle will do whatever we want," Carlos says.

"Will they let me see their music video?"

"Which one? We've made ten of twelve tracks. Not that they're up and running."

"Not up and running? It's on all the time, Carlos," Maggie says.

"You mean, *you* play it all the time!" Carlos says. "You spend hours locked in your room with it."

"What does it matter?" I say. "What do we care about rights, royalties, and profits? We're indifferent to money and power, privilege and prestige."

"Oh, I know that," Maggie says. "It's just that *some* of us are more indifferent than others."

I've dropped my Diva Savior act (I think). At least, I'm not teasing them when I say, "All I've ever wanted is to reach something higher. To put my finger on one ideal outside the normal scope." My feeling is sincere, and yet, I am still on the balcony. I've hopped back onto the railing as morning zephyrs flutter my shirttails and ruffle my hair.

And Carlos laughs. "You really are too much. Come inside."

So, we proceed through the balcony doors and I sit at my desk. Maggie leans over, and fondly slips a lock of my hair behind my ear. "It's a *great* video, Malkie. You're going to love it."

"It's very respectful and…um, uplifting," Carlos says, circling behind me and resting his hands on my shoulders. "It's got Letitia Wright." He massages my neck. "Do you want to watch it?" He slips his hands down the front of my shirt, "I'll call it up." The reference points on my chest come to life beneath his fingertips.

And that does it! I shove him off of me. "Touch me again, Carlos," I levitate with outrage, "and I'll kill you! I *know* it's got Letitia Wright! I'm not insensate!"

Suddenly all subservient, Carlos bends at the waist and backs toward the door. But, I don't know, once I let him get to me, there's no peaceable way out. Swinging around, I grab him by the neck. "We own our own thoughts!" I yell in his face, as if this were a major point of contention. "We own our own fate!" My saliva flies at him. "We are all accountable," I practically spit, dragging him on to the floor.

"Yes, well—" Carlos grunts as I bounce on his chest, my nightshirt riding up.

"Yes, what?" I demand.

"Yes, well," Carlos sneers half in pain, half in disdain, "yes and no."

"*Well, yes and no?*" Does he always have to ridicule me? His life's in my hands! A shift of position and I could tear his balls off! A little pressure to his throat and he'd suffocate. And *still* he has to deride me! I grab his ears, preparing to beat his head against the floor.

"You-hoo!" Maggie calls from a distance. "You-hoo! Guys! This isn't helping!"

And, it seems, just before I can process her voice, a terrifying, wonderful, awful opportunity surfaces, wherein anything could happen—anything meaning murder. The word doesn't register, just the cold kernel of evil as I imagine slamming Carlos's head on the floor, his spine cracking, his neck a rope fraying between my fists. Except, of course, once Maggie speaks, the moment turns to scalding shame. I let go— and stand huffing by myself in the corner. Carlos leans unharmed against the doorframe and Maggie sits clutching a pillow.

I was not, and am not—the last thing I will ever be—is sorry. But despite myself, the next words out of my mouth are: "I'm sorry, Carlos."

"Come downstairs," he says. "We'll watch the video."

"No, I don't think so; I'm no longer interested." The last thing I want at this point is to watch myself in full regalia, cresting before an awe-struck crowd, Louie and Lyle jamming, and Letitia Wright's unearthly voice wafting forth. With her singing behind me, my words could be gibberish and people would swear solidarity.

Carlos is talking but I can't hear him. "Pray tell," he asks, "no longer interested?"

"I—I'm just not up to it." I shake my head, flicking beads

of sweat into orbit. I lie on the bed overcome with thirst. (I really cannot go on; the chasm between now and *now* is just too jagged, too deep and dizzying for me to bridge.)

"Don't worry about the video," Maggie says, patting my ankle. "It's not a big deal."

"Correct me if I'm wrong," Carlos says, aching for more of a fight. "But I *told* you, not asked you, to come downstairs and see it."

"Whoa, ho—big, big Daddy!" I bolt up, restored by indignation. "Maggie's right—I'm the dog; she's the groomer; and you *think* you're my owner!" Finger to the wind, I mimic him, "*Correct* me if I'm wrong..." I shimmy at him, butt wagging, *good doggie, down doggie.*

Carlos, bear in mind, is small. And I am big. He's old and wrinkled and I am smooth and, still, by most lights in my prime. And so, just to show him how far-fetched his delusions are, I crawl and growl. "It's so much fun when you play master." I sit up, tongue hanging, and stroke my neck. ≈

Mad About the Boy

For two weeks, I've stared into space, too listless to read or write. I've lolled in bed or the bathtub. I haven't done a meeting since my attack of aphasia (or whatever-it-was) before the idolizing crowd prostrating itself at my feet.

Carlos runs the meetings now. Carlos runs everything. And evidently Carlos has decided to leave me to my own devices. When I'm not just staring or lolling, I read a book, a big, fat biography of Leonardo da Vinci. But I can't go out. I cannot leave this room unless I want to face a handful of supplicants bowing and scraping, weeping and wailing for miracles I cannot even pretend to perform.

If it weren't for Maggie, I don't know what. She comes by to check on me once or twice a day—I'm sure with Carlos's bidding. I'm guessing he wants me distraught and off balance, but not stark raving insane.

So Maggie visits, bearing little snippets from the outside. She tells me about the promos and follow-ups and some of Carlos's machinations. She praises my discipline toward the purification regimen we've both adopted. We drink ten glasses of mineral water and rub alpha hydroxyl lotion into our skin. Maggie and I are nothing if not intimates.

And I confide in her: "I can't spend the rest of my life in isolation. This whole thing is temporary. It has to be."

"Of course it is," Maggie says.

But I'm not reassured. Because of something in her voice? Or, something in mine? *Is my isolation temporary?* Changing tacks, I ask delicately: "*So*, Maggie, who's coming to Carlos's multimedia things?"

—And to her predictable reply, I say, "*Of course* a lot of people. I know that much. My question is, are they the same people from one night to the next?"

—And here again, trying to hurry through the maddening preliminaries, I nod: Yes, I know we're holding meetings at several locations, and no, I never imagined she attended all of them. "But at the ones you *do* attend, are there any noticeable regulars?"

"Like who?"

"Like I don't know…" I suck my fingernail. "You must have *some* impression."

She shakes her head.

"When you're at the meetings, have you ever noticed, say, one particular person?"

"What kind of person, Malkie?"

"Just anyone that stands out."

"Let me think." She taps her temple. "Have I ever noticed anyone standing out?"

"Just forget it."

"No…now that you mention it—" She's really enjoying this. "There is *one* person…"

My hands fly up to cover my ears. "No!"

"But Malcolm, you *asked*! What's the matter with you?"

Where is the boy? How can I find him? My thinking so manifest a blind person could see it, a deaf one hear it—I pull away. But Maggie sticks her nose right up underneath mine. "Come on, Malkie," she insists. "This is Maggie you're talking to."

All right, I think, it can't hurt to try. Going for a detached tone, I ask, "Do you know if anyone's heard from Mad Mike?"

"Mad Mike? Is *that* who you're interested in?"

"No. Of course not. Just forget I said anything."

"If you want out of your tower of isolation…"

"Leave me alone! Okay? I don't care anymore!"

My hands clench and my head burns, but as she's closing the door, she flashes me a sad, wistful little smile. ≈

Beautiful Boys in Berets

Today, I'm ready for her. I've been up all night, waiting to show her what I can do. And so naturally she doesn't come at dawn, or at ten, or even at noon. This only reinforces my premonition. For once I am flush not with remorse—but success!

You see, last night, (I leave my confines when everyone sleeps), I discovered a cache of Carlos's stuff. He keeps his inner sanctum locked, but at two in the morning I happened upon a storage box in a third-floor closet. Lifting a cardboard flap, I found the embroidered boxes with the Chinese iron balls. First separately, then in pairs, I rolled them in my hands. They felt heavier than I expected, cool and smooth, and my coordination with them waxed and waned. I'd no sooner find a rhythm than I'd lose it. But at dawn, with Maggie due to witness it, the technique blossomed in me. Mysteriously simple, it possessed me, and yet, I possessed it. And I wasn't about to put it down just because Maggie was off-schedule.

At two in the afternoon she finally poked her head in.

Still aswirl in my happy aperture, I straightened my arms, showing her the iron balls going clockwise in my left hand, counterclockwise in my right.

"Hey," she said, "not bad." And we both sort of snorted. My little show of manipulating two pairs of iron balls—and at the same time, talking, struck me as comical. "The thing I've been meaning to ask you," I reversed the balls' orbits perfectly and then, shit, lost just enough concentration to bungle where my questions were going. "Do any of the people at Carlos's meetings," the words were out of my mouth before I could stop them, "wear berets?"

"Berets?" She had to check my face; it was too good to be true. "I can find out."

"No." The orbs chimed in sync. "Don't bother."

"I won't *bother*, I'll just ask Carlos how many followers wear berets."

"You can't. It's ridiculous." And for one transcendent moment (in which you'd think I'd know enough to consider myself warned), I felt fantastically composed. As if the spinning balls cast a whispery truth: as if I, Malcolm Tully, for one sublime second could do no wrong. "It's just that for a while there it seemed like maybe a trend was starting."

"A beret trend?" Maggie giggled. And with this, the field surrounding me disintegrated. The iron balls were still chiming, but I was clearly mistaken about no false moves. *A beret trend?* I was way, way up there, without a 'chute.

"Yeah, well, kind of a fad." My fingers worked faster. I cleared my throat and said, "For a while there it seemed like…" (I can hardly write this without exhorting myself to stop! Shut up!) "half the guys at the meetings wore long hair and berets."

"Really," Maggie said, "long hair and berets. Were these young guys?"

"A little," I said. "A little on the young side."

"And beautiful? Beautiful slender young guys with huge eyes and cheekbones and mouths like Johnny Depp's?"

"I didn't say that!" My voice bounced from a shout to a hiss then back to a shout. "Maggie! I didn't *say* that!" I could feel my face contorting, little involuntary muscles jerking. "And you *know it!*"

"Honestly, Malcolm!" She was laughing. "You think I didn't notice the beautiful boy in the beret among Mad Mike's crew? And then when he came to a few meetings? Why, I was right in there with you, babe, drooling all over him." ≈

Idiotic But Unignorable

Of course, Maggie noticed him. With the crew. Without the crew. In meetings. Not in meetings. She's not blind.

"So," she pats my hand. "What do you want to know?"

His name is Tyler Dineen. And he won't turn twenty until February. He dropped out of Northwestern after three semesters, just like me. But not, like me, because of a tragedy. More like Maggie, because he had no idea who he was or what he wanted to be—only what he did *not* want to be: Not, Maggie says, a drone or a whore. Or, should that prove impossible, Tyler at least didn't want to be one of them for very long. So Mad Mike hired him as a favor to Tyler's aunt, a lawyer who frequently gets Mad Mike free from charges of illegal possession.

"And now," Maggie says, "now that Mad Mike's drying out at the clinic in Minnesota, the young and beautiful Tyler is working as a bike messenger."

"Maggie," I say, "how do you know?"

"I know. I have his cell number."

His cell number? All these weeks of suspension, of stasis, of hoping, praying that somehow, someday, my formless, flummox-addled life might coincide with one more glimmering moment of his: It's too stupid, too pathetically banal. I can't stand it: *His cell phone number!*

Only the oblique logic that since this angelic boy and I met once, we must therefore meet again has gotten me—barely—through airless, meaningless days and ridiculously formatted nights. The meetings, the signings. The ersatz benedictions. The ever widening, weeks-on-end isolation. If it weren't for Tyler asking me, Blunt in hand among the ruins of my one true shop, *did I mind?*, surely I would have lost my mind. Had I not recognized his luminous face in the dark and bobbling sea of blissed-out bodies, had I not dreamed of…

Maggie's staring at me, and I'm staring into space. An untraceable alarm, from a car or clock somewhere, startles me. I flinch and feel a tremor underfoot, as if the energy at the source of everything just dropped a notch. I swallow hard.

Maggie's saying, "Earth to Malcolm!"

"Malkie!" Maggie calls. "Come and sit down."

She smooths my hair; she makes little shush-shush sounds. We're rocking together on the window seat. She says, "What if we say this: You don't have to call him or anything. I'll do it."

"Don't."

"Why not?"

"Because, you can't. Because you have no idea what's at stake."

"This is *Maggie*—"

"I know who you are." Too agitated to sit, I'm up now, and pacing.

"Malcolm—"

"There's no way it'll make sense to you; it doesn't make sense to me. The situation is so absurd. Contacting that boy would be like grave digging. Ghoulish and futile—and wrong!"

"Tyler Dineen," she says, "is someone you could really help. He's working as a bike messenger because he's smart enough to realize if you do one thing for too long, it takes over. You're stuck. Now if you could just get *yourself* unstuck from your own bizarro obsessions a minute, you could show him how to be. It's like if you put your mind to it, you could help this kid exactly the way hundreds of your followers imagine you help them. *You could be for real, Malkie!*"

"Oh God, Maggie, don't say that."

"Why not?"

My head is cooked, listening to her. And to reorient myself, I estimate the number of telemarketers downstairs, the followers in the prayer room, and of course, the customers, the baker-novitiates, acolytes and waitresses. Greg's blue-eyed deaf white cat is napping in my laundry hamper. An ocean CD plays in one room, Thelonious Monk in another. The windows are open and a misty drizzle is falling.

"What if you and Tyler and I meet for lunch someday?" Maggie says. "The three of us can exchange pleasantries over salad niçoise."

Listening to the undertones, the stifled music beneath, I say, "He's a teenager."

"Yeah, well, so are a lot of people. That's why you've got to normalize your relations and get *out* now and then."

I'm nodding and mouthing the words, "All right, Maggie."

"And," she says, "extreme case, if this is some monumental spiritual test, you'll pass it!"

"I will?"

"Yes."

"I suppose," I say haltingly, "if…if it's really meant to be —I can't run away." I say this but I don't believe it. The ambient sounds fade to a high-pitched stream of air that's almost humorous, like some goofy kid's whistling. There's an echo of myself saying, *I can't run away.* And I think, *well, I ought to: I'm not paralyzed.* Whereupon I internally stumble into the terrible, unthinkable. The thing I'm always running away from, just never fast or far enough:

> *If only instead of standing there, mouth open, soundlessly screaming No No No, if only I'd jumped! Jumped to keep him from jumping!*

I can't sit in my room. I can't go out. I can't run away.

Maggie's saying, "Balance. We need to achieve balance." But she's not really here. This is fill-in time. In the waiting area.

> *I knew it was coming! I knew! I knew that night, under the chandelier, up the fire escape, onto the roof. I knew! Every sip of champagne, every particle of light. I knew how quickly rapture turns to pain! How despair thrives inside happiness! I knew how powerful and uncontrollable the two of us were.*

How total to the point of blackout our daily, nightly, transports were. Stop, oh stop, it's killing me, *I screamed. Yet Colin and I never shied or slowed. I could feel the lethal factor everywhere. But young and in love, I didn't care. We laughed like fools—there were no limits.*

This is the aftermath of that. And now, Christ—it's so totally incongruous!—there is this idiotic, but unignorable talisman, a look-alike boy and his cell phone number! ≈

Goodbye, Maggie

October 9

Apparently I freaked Maggie out. She knocked on my door this morning, before six, a huge maroon garment bag hanging from one shoulder, a big black suitcase on wheels by her feet. "Hi," she said, striding into the room, brisk with purpose. "I'm going on a little business trip."

"Religion Without Rules business?"

"Yes," she draped the garment bag over a chair and stood in the middle of the room, rubbing her hands together. "I'll be gone a couple of weeks. Maybe a little more, depending on how things go."

"What things?"

"Carlos wants me to go to L.A. and see about setting up a center there."

"Yeah well, have fun."

"Malkie, I'll miss you as much as you miss me." She put her hands on my shoulders. "Maybe more."

"Maybe less." I backed away and more or less shrugged. ≈

Wishful Thinking

I keep reminding myself, everything's fine, everything's good: I've got everything anyone could possibly want. Money, fame, sex, and song. Legions to do my bidding. And for the first time in my life I am—icing on the cake here—effortlessly slim. No tricky diets, no arduous exercises. Plain, hard faith gets you abs of steel.

My secular beliefs, as in—*Maggie will come home; Tyler will sit at my feet and I'll want nothing more. Colin's memory will fill me with purity*—are beyond question. So why not concentrate on the present? Which is: "Oh wow, my very own cult!" ≈

Going Through the Motions

October 18

Three times this week I've appeared live and impromptu downstairs, trying with all my might not to put on airs. I made my appearances during our main bakery's lull, about 2:30 p.m. And yet, even with a half dozen people there, the moment I materialize, everyone falls silent. Such a pall of expectation fills the room that standing there, in broad daylight, I have to reevaluate how to be. Who, honestly, do I think I am?

Maggie does not call or write and I'm too angry to e-mail her.

This past week has left me even more lost than before. A typical day involves *a lot* of sleep. And when I awake, a lot of anxious, prescient daydreaming. A few hours online, a few hours reading until the dead, dead of night, which is the only time (not counting those three anomalies) I dare to roam the building.

And if, perchance, I encounter an all-night disciple, I instinctively perform a half-hearted bow, followed by my fingers traveling to the person's forehead. Once or twice, I opted for a regular handshake, but it simply did not suffice. Better to touch their temples than to have them pound their noses at my feet.

In any event, when I meet someone face to face, a spontaneous little ceremony erupts: heads down, eyes together, away. The tap to the forehead came about, I think, as a signal to move on. ≈

Om

October 19

For a change of pace, I've decided to try roller blading. And in the afternoon? Fly fishing, tap dancing, what's the difference? Officially, I'm meditating. Not fuming that Maggie's abandoned me. Not fighting back tears over the extravagancy of relinquishing this moment for the next, that moment for the one just past.

Appearances to the contrary:

I am meditating.

I am focusing on *OM.* ≈

Not That It Matters

I can't believe she hasn't sent me one fucking sentence. Not one postcard of Hollywood. Not one: "Wish you were here." Tuesday I broke down and e-mailed her: *Tell me what's up.* And has she, *has* she? No! She has not bothered to tap back so much as: *Not much.*

Which, I wonder, would be worse: asking Carlos, "Heard anything from Maggie?" Or not asking him.

This afternoon, I've silently rehearsed putting the question to Stephanie, Annick, Morgan, Sylvia, Rafe, Graham, Elise, Greg, fill in the blank: *Oh by the way, Fill-in-the-blank, do you know when Maggie's due back? Is it this month or next? Not that it matters.*

Why should it? ≈

Carlos Did This

She said she'd be gone a couple of weeks. Well, it's *been* a couple of weeks. So maybe she's on a plane this minute.

Okay, I tell myself. Be big. Be brave. Can't you go a few weeks without her holding your hand? My strategy is to wait and see. (If doing nothing can be called a strategy.)

I'm sure Carlos knows where Maggie is and how long she'll be there. But I've decided I absolutely cannot ask him. For no one knows better than Carlos that I cannot go on without her! And he deliberately set this up! How can I call for help, when the only one to hear me is the guy trying to do me in? ≈

That's What Religions Do

This morning—a change. An occasion. Something real for me to do. Carlos is interviewing acolytes for a new managerial position, head of operations, and he wants me to stand by as an enticement. (The applicants are all dying to shake my hand, don'tcha know? And, it goes without saying, glad to work for a pittance.) I look at him, ready to barter: *Want me to stand by, Carlos? Then tell me when Maggie's coming home.* But a terrible new dread emanates from him, an ashen, ready-to-fall-apart quality that leaves me mumbling half of I wanted to say: "Just tell me when."

"Now," Carlos says. "Sit by the window. And just—lend your presence." His head whips around, and the tension rippling from him is palpable. He pinches his nose and rubs his eyes as a bouncy disciple named Jocelyn ushers in the first applicant.

Bob Morris with orangish tufts growing from symmetrical patches on his head shakes Carlos's hand and half genuflects at me. His clothes look like prototypes of permanent press and he sprays saliva with the first words out of his mouth. Carlos looks over Bob Morris's resumé, slips it into a folder, and asks Bob where he sees himself in ten years. (Now *that's* pure Carlos, but when I catch his eye, there's no mirth.) Fifteen unironic minutes later Carlos races through the same routine with Keith Cormier, an overweight thirty-year-old with an associate degree who claims Religion Without Rules has cured him of alcoholism.

Next comes Jenny Gentile, a pale, sturdy, woman in her forties. Before she's hardly sat down, one of our financial-tier lovelies interrupts. Carlos excuses himself ("Talk to her, Malcolm. Share your wisdom,") and confers with the dazzling young man in the hall.

I hear anger in Carlos's voice. "Shit!" A flash of disbelief. *"What in Christ?"* And as the large pale woman in front of me tells me she has an MBA from Circle Campus, Carlos is in the hallway hissing, "What the fuck is going on?"

The woman, whose teeth are tiny and coffee stained, tells me she wants this job. She has to get this job. She'll do anything.

"Would you say you were born to do it?"

"Yes. Absolutely. I was born to do it."

"Then the job is yours."

I stand up to shake her hand as Carlos, now half in the office, half in the hallway, says, "Got that? If Credit Suisse calls, I'm unavailable."

The ponytailed Adonis mumbles and Carlos snarls, " —tell them if they can't wait a week, they can all go to hell!"

Then he turns to us, saying, "Well," with forced cheeriness, "what can you do?" Our newly hired operations manager prepares to run through her credentials again. I can see it on her face, so I intervene. "I gave Ms. Gentile the job, Carlos. We shook hands."

He dips his head, which appears to be plastered with sweat. "What can any of us do," he asks, "but grit our teeth and go through the motions?"

"I don't know," Jenny says.

And Carlos nods. "If you want to do your own paperwork, you can start tomorrow. Otherwise we're waiting for Maggie to get back, first week in November."

And I'm out of my seat, *"The first week in November, Carlos?* God damn it, what's taking so long?" I'm boring in on him. "Did you send her away just to drive me nuts? Did you? If this is another one of your force-feed, deprivation techniques, I don't need it. I'll do what you want, Carlos. Just tell me! You win!"

"Malcolm, please!" Carlos jerks, meaning, stop this in front of Ms. Gentile.

"My point exactly! You cannot afford to have me flip out, Carlos! You need me to stick to the designated continuum no matter what."

"Look, Malcolm, no one's depriving you of Maggie. She's interviewing people in L.A. She's setting up centers and establishing connections with the colleges there."

"Get a load of this guy—" my eyes roll around. "Do you believe him?" I ask our phlegmatic new manager. "Do you believe anyone in his right mind believes him?"

"Come around ten," Carlos whisks Jenny Gentile out the door, and calls down the hall. "Jocelyn, can you see our new operations manager the rest of the way out?"

Sweet young Jocelyn bounces back into view. Carlos is chuckling as he closes the door behind them. But a second later, when I look up, he's hemming and hawing. "Um, Malcolm. We've, uh, well, we've expanded very rapidly. Starting tonight, we're going to have to go back to our original format..." (He's so nervous he's chewing the tips of his mustache!) "Where you lead the meetings. Without the charisma of you in the pulpit, in the flesh, we have nothing. We need your divine energy to keep things rolling."

"Divine energy, Carlos? Isn't that laying it on a little thick? We must be in some deep shit."

He wags a finger. "Now, now. 'Darkest before the dawn.' And, I want you to know Maggie's business in California is very, very important. We've reached the stage," so concerned he's whispering, Carlos jams his hands into his pockets, "where we need to recruit people who are qualified to work as ministers in other cities."

"Why?" It dawns on me—in fact it's high noon and blazing on me—that things are out of control.

"Because before the year is out, we're going to have centers in L.A. and San Francisco." His voice changes, off the cuff. "And then Seattle and Vancouver. Houston, Miami, and Key West."

(And, you know how one minute you're saying one thing, and then suddenly you're in lock step with what one *might say*? *Mightn't one now*? Well, here comes Cary Grant addressing

Carlos): "All going smoothly, I trust? Finding the communications majors you need to fill the ranks?"

"I think so," he says. "California is half way there. And before Christmas we should be up and running in Texas and Florida."

"Really?"

"And then probably D.C. and Baltimore."

"Really," I say. "Just the U.S., Carlos? Not Paris, London, Rome? Not Cairo, Calcutta, Tokyo?"

"Next year," he says.

And I'm like, oh! "So that's your ultimate goal. To take over the world!"

"We've started a religion," Carlos says flatly. "and that's what religions do." ≈

Just Blow on Them, Carlos

October 28

Tall, dark, graceful Greg no longer works the cash register. He now works directly with Carlos. It could just be me, but it certainly seems that Carlos the Unshakable *trembles* as Greg comes and goes on various errands. Greg glides by, Carlos's eyes soften, his mouth slackens.

I've noticed other things, too. Carlos grits his teeth and rubs his eyes till they look red and bruised. On the phone more than ever, he rages under his breath. And when he thinks no one's looking he pops little peach-colored pills from his pockets, swallowing them dry. He smells like metal and Tic-tacs. And, now that I've started doing meetings again, his nimble fingers keep lighting on *me* again, deftly stroking my chest or neck until I brush them off. "That's over, Carlos!"

"Sorry," he says, "Natural reaction."

Oh, and another thing: He's rediscovered the iron balls, and works them constantly, around and around. But instead of casting a spell with them, as he did on me, I swear it's the opposite—Carlos is begging them to cast a spell on him. They spin and chime as fluently as ever, but he's like a gambler with dice. *Come on, little darlings, Poppa's baby needs new shoes.* ≈

I Want Every Moment Back

November 3

At daybreak, I watched from my balcony as the top of Greg's gleaming brown head approached the soot-dusted Cherokee parked across the street. In the chill air, he blew on his hands before opening the door and driving away. At nine-thirty a.m., staring (still or again?) through the balcony doors, I noticed the same dirty car pull in front of the shop and let Maggie out. I sighed and paced, alarmed, yes, but not out of control. I heard through the floorboards a round of hellos and Roger offering to take her suitcases.

Then I heard her laugh: five alto trills. A graceful fading that led to a pause I couldn't interpret: embarrassment, apology? Or just a gaze around the shop. Who was with her? I heard various mumblings followed by that musical half-scale of hers again, a bit higher, louder, happier.

And then—suddenly, she was skipping up the back stairs. I heard her hesitate at my door...*You can do this!* She knocked! *She won't know anything you don't tell her.* She said, "Malkie!" *So don't say a thing!* "Malkie, open up." *Don't!* But of course I opened the door, with a forced sing-song of, "Mag-gie!"

We both stared at our feet until I couldn't stand it, and blushing horribly, tried this: "Is it just me or what? Remember when people would say that?"

She smiled, answering, "When I was fourteen, I said, *'Is it just me or what?'* And, *'Whatever.'* And, *'As if.'* "

" *'As if'* came later, I think."

We hugged. I pressed my cheek into her hair, which wasn't as blonde as I remembered it, but much softer and straighter, smooth and reassuring. A veil of pure silk dried in balmy air after a fresh rain. I rubbed my cheek there and my hand played with the feminine waves. A sigh escaped and she pulled away. "I missed you, too, Malkie."

"Holding her shoulders, I said, "Why didn't you call? Write? You must have known how it would be here, how Carlos would be, without you here."

"Malkie, I am sorry about that." She turned red and squirmed and I released my hands from her shoulders. "I am *really* sorry. Do you forgive me?"

For what? I tried to say. *For what?* The most I could muster was a weak shrug.

"I shouldn't have stayed away so long. I should have written; I should have called. But I'll make it up to you. I'll tell you everything."

"That's okay. Carlos explained everything."

"He did? How?"

"It's enough that you're back."

"I'll make it up to you. You'll see. Everything's going to be the same as before."

"I know." And then explaining it was time for my shower, I hurried her out.

*

I never know what's going to bring on a crying jag. *"Is it just me or what?"* was never, before or after its currency, said in earnest. People never said it unless they were referring to something indisputable, guaranteed to draw consensus.

So which do you think? Is it just me or does the irreversibility of time never let up? Is it just me or are there days when you, too, can't get past every moment lost? I want every moment back: The good because they passed too fast, and the bad because perhaps with another chance, I could make them right. ≈

We Hate to Be Reminded

November 6

Now that Maggie's back, our one unstated, mutual goal is to avoid each other. We were—or no, not we, I—I was so intimate with her: Dream-wise, heart-, soul- and trust-wise—no boundaries! Anything Maggie wanted to see, I showed. *Be with me and be my guest* was how I was with her. Give, give, give: I let her read my mind, explore my feelings, gauge my desires. For free! *Step right up, Maggie Townsend, stay as long as you want, and then? Cut and run. No risk, no obligation.*

Oh, I know, it was fun at the time. And the one-way aspect is not entirely her fault. I was the focus, the touch point of otherworldliness. By all rights, she may well blame me for never looking into the fabric of *her* soul. But she was the psychic nursemaid, I was the holy child, and the whole thing was finally, obviously, a very sick joke. That's why we dread seeing each other—it's shamefully but finally over, and we hate to be reminded. ≈

My Turn to Laugh (1)

Just after eleven last night, Carlos knocks on my door. I shut my book. When Maggie was gone, I began to reread big portions of the great novels. *The Brothers Karamazov. Crime and Punishment. The Idiot* (with which I naturally identify). I have a lot of time on my hands and the books calm me down after the meetings and signings and other nonsense. Now I'm into Nabokov: *Pale Fire*.

We smile—instantly naughty, giddy, complicit with each other. The man does know how to work me; give him that. Carlos is standing there, barefoot, in a deep red, absurdly elegant cashmere smoking outfit, with claret- and black-striped satin lapels. I think, Halloween? No, that was last week. And the idea that he's dressed up like this for me expands in my chest, a helium ball of delight. And, as if that weren't enough, he puts on a show of flexing his sensuous strong brown feet, rocking from ball to heel. Rhythmically.

"Oh, pretty good," I concede, taking a step back. "What else can you do—just for me? A pirouette?"

"But of course. I would whether you asked or not." Nose in the air, he turns, bows, and twirls around twice before presenting the bottle of Yquem. He's cradling the wine in one arm, and dangling from his other hand a pair of clinking crystal wine glasses, stems entwined with his fabulous fingers.

"To what," I ask, "do I owe the pleasure?"

"Can I come in?"

"Yes, come in, and tell me, why are you doing this?"

"Religion Without Rules," he opens the Yquem, "is entering a phase of profound flux."

He pours the golden wine into the goblets. We raise them for a salutary clinking, but I stop. "Profound flux? Does that mean celebration or a shutdown or both?"

"A shutdown?" Carlos's mouth tightens. "No. Nothing like that. Think of it as a changing of the guard."

"Oh?" The wine is sweet and I shut my eyes upon each sip.

"It's time for me to step down, Malcolm, or at least back."

"Oh, really?"

"I'm not walking away; you can't get rid of me that easily. *But:* it's time for you to assume control. You're the one, Malcolm. I don't belong at the steering wheel."

"Ah-ha! Ah-ha!" We're in really deep shit, but I knew that already. Taking hold of Carlos's wrists, I learn, from his pulse, the cast of his eyes, the barely perceptible twitching of his flat cheeks and still dark, thick, but dry lips, something I wouldn't have guessed: Not that he's afraid—of course he is, but so what? Rather, he's lost his own game and he knows it.

My turn to laugh!

He breaks from my hands and parades the length of the room. Shoulders back, hands accentuating his svelte waist, he steps high and pivots. He sashays. And just when I'm thinking well, maybe he's not totally out of play—my God! Carlos goes down on one knee. Facing me, he bows and rubs his gray head. He raises brimming dark eyes, and pleads, his raspy voice wavering, for just one more time with me. My terms, however I want it, me on top, or him. He won't ask again, "Please!"

Of course, I knew better. But with the wine, the jacket, Carlos's incredible *gestures*, how could I say no? It was just this once, never again, what the hell? ≈

My Turn to Laugh (2)

All through the night, until early this morning, the final-final:

My great lacquer bed at sea in the room, I pull out and kneel up, off of him. Rolling Carlos onto his back, I lower myself flush on top of his spare, delicate old frame. Intertwining our fingers, I push his arms up over his head. "Now you have to swear this was the last time."

"This was the last time."

"Why?" I quiz him. "Why can it never happen again?"

"Because you say so."

"Very good, Carlos." I pull the sheet between us and wedge a pillow under his back. "But what else?"

"From now on," Carlos says, "I have to do what you say."

"Or else what?"

"Or else you'll leave me."

"Yes, Carlos. But what if I leave you anyway?"

"You can't," he says. "You won't."

"Neither of us knows that." Turning away and bounding up, I slip into some clothes Maggie chose for me—when?

Months ago. Somehow during this last spate of desolation, my lank dark hair has grown long and wildly lustrous.

"Amazing," Carlos says as I toss it back, out of my way.

"If I weren't so benevolent," I say, "I'd make you crawl."

This is too much, and we both start to laugh. Carlos, reverting to form, harrumphs, "Yeah, right." Except instantly then, the new, more submissive guy is back: Lying on his side, hand propping his head, Carlos picks at the sheet, stares at his fingers, and mumbles. Of course he *is* still Carlos with the same old complaint. It's just that instead of shaking his fist in anger, he's whining! "For six years, I did all the work and you bagged the money. And now, for ten minutes—our roles get switched."

"Ten minutes, Carlos? You'd die if I left!"

Sitting up cross-legged, naked, old Carlos or new, I can't really tell, shrugs this off, as if, so what, why should he care? Alive or dead, it's all the same to him.

"Don't be ridiculous." I say, heading for the door. "You'd die if I left! You can't live without me!" The situation couldn't be plainer: I'm on top; I have the advantage. But—it's taking me forever to cross the room.

I hate to look; and yet—I cannot not look: Carlos is getting dressed. In this light, my lust slaked, I can see how shorn and skinny he is, how hairless and withered. *So leave the room, Malcolm.* But, my God, there's no escaping it. Awkward, unsatisfying, infinitely lamentable—no matter what I say, it's not completely over. Repercussions are camping out around the block.

I was almost out the door, home free, when I stopped and

turned around. Because there was that finger-snapping sensation. That *wait a minute, what've-I-forgotten?* hesitation that's impossible to ignore.

So back in the room, arms folded, I huff and puff: "All right, what is it?"

And Carlos tosses his head, saying, "Go away, Malcolm. Just like that—walk away now that you've stolen my identity."

"Oh please—"

"You're hanging around to see how close I'll come."

"Carlos, I know about the money. You knew that, right? How many shops, how many mortgages? And, oh, yes, the stock market. You better get me performing in big-city arenas. Nonstop. Simulcast everywhere."

"It's not really that bad," Carlos says. "I've got some of the best financial minds in the country advising us. And both of them think, basically, things will work out."

"You're so full of shit, Carlos. There's no scenario, no restructuring that can save you if I decide to walk. If I skip out on you, Carlos, the whole thing will come crashing down within days!"

"Okay," he rushes over to me. A web of involuntary muscles throbs under his skin. "There may have been a few bad investments. One or two overly optimistic projections. But I've got things under control now."

"It's sad, really," I start to say. "the way you're always lying to yourself. Our creditors are going to hunt you down—" The words are lining up on the tip of my tongue, and then, I don't know, a signal flashes. Something displaces me. *"They'll break your neck. They'll ruin you—"*

Did I say it out loud? All I know is a flash of static shoots between us, and then, will wonders never cease? Carlos lays a solicitous—not a creepy, not what you'd expect—hand on my shoulder. "Nonstop praying," he says, "takes a toll."

And then I remember: Two or three years ago I foresaw our present exchange exactly as it just happened. I know déjà vu is supposedly just a neuron misfiring. But *why* is it misfiring? Why then? Why now? I *am remembering.*

It was before Christmas and Carlos had made a whole village of chocolate-covered meringue we were going to display in front. He had labored all day with an intensity of purpose that even then I found intimidating. And while in those days our relationship was perfectly ordinary, I remember watching him roll down his sleeves, and feeling shocked, as if someone had spilled a cup of hot water down my front.

Looking over his shoulder, he whisked off his apron, and spoke the exact words he just said: *Nonstop praying takes a toll.*

Years ago, this expression came to me on a raft of desire and discomfort. I knew I'd remember it.

Altogether my recollection of a future-recollection lasts as long as a long, drawn out, almost discounted *Ah-Choo!* Two more quick little sneezes, and I'm out the door, ready for I don't know what. ≈

No One Gets Out Alive

November 12

Carlos asked Stephanie to drive in from Lincoln Park. We needed to go over stuff. No longer dour or drab, Stephanie parked a shiny red car directly beneath the conference room's windows. I waved from above and whistled in appreciation when she flounced in, all feathery new hairstyle and aggressively gold jewelry. A skinny, inconspicuous acolyte brought in a tray of Lapsang Soochong, oranges, and almond crescent cookies. Carlos ordered him to close the door. And then, although the acolyte had left and the latch had clicked, Carlos fumed, stirring the air so we all knew how severely, how seriously he was fuming. "First off," he said, "I want to know if we can double next week's schedule."

"And I want to know," Stephanie wasted no time, "who's buying me out?"

Carlos glowered theatrically. "I told you on the phone: we're not going to get into that now."

"Oh yeah? Well, I need the money now."

Carlos rose in his seat. "This is not the time nor the place for this conversation, and if you persist in talking about it, Stephanie, I promise you: You will regret it."

I smirked at her, expecting her to say something like, "Persist, I must, my good fellow." You know, something droll. But she was seething. Her whole outline rippled—the momentarily glamorous Stephanie changing into a woman so enraged as to make the glum old Stephanie blanch. "You honestly think I drove down here to help you iron out the performance schedule?"

Carlos said, "Malcolm, will you excuse us?"

But Stephanie said, "No! Stay here!" She folded her arms, and laughed. "Carlos, you couldn't possibly have thought this would go down any differently than it *is* going down. As we speak."

"I'm afraid," Carlos said, "you're making it highly unlikely that you and I will ever reach an equitable agreement."

"You don't have a choice."

"Nor do you."

Stephanie slammed her china tea cup hard on its saucer. "You're the one who'll be sorry," she said, as the cup cracked into jagged, steaming shards. Eyes never leaving Carlos's, she carefully extricated her fingers, removing the broken-off handle like a ring from her index finger. "The truth will out!"

Carlos called in another acolyte to clean up the mess, and then sank back miserably, shaking his head. "You know, ultimately, it's all going to go to a bunch of lawyers." He cast me a woeful glance and I could not tell, even when he brightened maniacally, whether his behavior was premeditated.

"You know, Steph? Why didn't *I* think of this?" he whooped. "Malcolm *should* know what you're forcing us into!"

And here he switched from talking ostensibly to Stephanie, to ostensibly me, but really, to himself. "In fact, how could I have been so blind? Your allegiance, Malcolm, is the ultimate factor."

*

Stephanie, it turned out, was insisting Religion Without Rules buy back her house for the price she paid, plus what she and Rafe had put into it. A sum Carlos called "beyond obscene," but Stephanie declared the least she deserved, considering she was, don't forget, a founding partner. Rafe, of course, was entitled to half of the house. But the Belden Avenue bakery was *hers*. To dissolve her stake completely, she wanted sole ownership.

Apparently, Stephanie and Rafe had been renovating a 1920s house they'd bought on Geneva Terrace. And in place of non-supporting walls, they'd installed 750 cubic feet of customized salt-water aquariums.

"Why, why, why," Carlos said, "being the big question."

"It was Rafe's idea. Based on the Doctrine and a soupçon of yin-yang."

"And just where is Rafe?" Carlos asked.

"Agree to my terms and maybe I'll tell you."

"Where?" Carlos pounded the table. "Again? Stephanie?"

"God, don't have a heart attack. He's with some friends who I think are deprogrammers."

"Deprogrammers? You mean cult specialists?"

"By day they're carpenters working on extra floor support. But I, in any case, am getting out."

With the idea of Stephanie (of anyone) *getting out*, a luminous chink opened in me. The possibility of *sole ownership of one shop* transformed night into day.

Carlos said, "No one can do anything for two months."

"Why, why, why," Stephanie said, "being the big question."

"In two months, we'll be fully liquid. Plus Malcolm, if you can double the meetings and éclair ceremonies, do some pay TV, stuff like that, we'll set up a safety net." He rubbed his eyes. "Here's what the financial advisors are telling me: Two months of positive cash flow and we're back in business, two months of peak capacity and we're home free."

"What?" The front legs of my chair hit the floor.

"We've hit a few snags." Carlos massaged his neck. "The stock market. The mortgages. The cash outlays. We'll be fine. This is a common side-effect of sudden growth."

Stephanie said, "I'm not waiting two weeks, let alone two months, Carlos. I'll be back tomorrow with my lawyer."

"You see? What did I tell you?" He threw up his hands. "It never fails. It all goes to the lawyers."

You have no idea how this bit of flirting with sell-offs and division cheered me! My smile so big it hurt, I said, "Stephanie, name your price. I'll buy your aquarium house for whatever you want."

Carlos said, "You can't! You have no idea what is going

on!" Tendons bulging from his neck, he slapped his palms on the table. "No one gets out alive!" He stood up and stuck his face an inch from mine, "Do you hear me? Meeting adjourned." ≈

Solemn and Absurd (1)

After Carlos stormed out, Stephanie tried to convince me that he was evil incarnate, ambition gone berserk, which I assured her I well knew. But—did I realize he'd sunk Religion Without Rules into an ocean of debt?

For all she knew, he was ignoring the taxes as well. What did I want to bet Carlos would get off scot-free? While I'd have to account for this mess the rest of my life?

And yet (she jabbed a finger in the air), for my personal prosperity and longevity, I owed it to myself to buy her house. Only because I was me could she let me have it for "half a million." Provided of course we legally transferred the Belden Avenue shop to her immediately.

"Don't you want to see the place?" Her hand came up near my cheek, and I watched her eyes shine with apparent fondness.

The last time Stephanie had touched me was that night Carlos came back after deserting me for three days. She'd put her arms around my middle and told me to go on out there and be a man, and her voice (which was not really her voice but *his*) made me buckle. And now, with her hand so near my face, I sputtered and burned. "Yeah, okay, let's go look at it."

*

One especially hot, dull, September afternoon, Maggie had wanted to show me Stephanie and Rafe's aquarium house. But I'd only gotten halfway to the car, because I wasn't up to people doing a double take: glancing at me, dismissing, then reconsidering: *Is that who I think it is?*

No! I would try to convey with a frown. *I'm nothing and no one!* Why would I lie?

But all it would take was one hesitant seeker to send me running back inside. Because I know too well what it's like: *Can I please make them rich? Beautiful? If they kneel down, can I make them love and be loved? If they prostrate themselves, say novenas, publish my favorite prayer in the newspaper, can I make their life a little better? What if they carve my name in their foreheads? Return every phone call, yield to every pedestrian? Can I then, if it's not too much trouble, just make everything not be so horrible all the time?*

I had scrambled back to my chambers, Maggie traipsing behind. One of these days, we'd try a stealth run in the middle of the night. If not next week, soon. Very soon.

Of course, now the idea of Maggie holding my hand, keeping the beggars at bay, makes me queasy with shame. Once she abandoned me, I realized how perverse—how utterly icky—my being her big baby actually is. A little revelation that has me more desperate than ever to get away.

With Stephanie ordinarily being such an uncongenial person, the near-miracle of her touch triggered a synaptic event: Head shooting flames, I intuitively leaped and spun through the realm of penitents, spiritual searchers, and vaguely threatening ascetics.

I bounced at the knees. I held out my arm to Stephanie. "Okay, I'm ready; let's go."

"Um," Stephanie said, "this baby-sitter's booked."

"What?"

"I promised my sister Marion I'd visit her in the nursing home this afternoon. Go and look around by yourself, with no anxious seller." She held out a key ring. "2317 Geneva Terrace, the silver key does the bottom lock, the gold the top."

"I don't know." I shook my head.

It's easy," Stephanie said. "Take the outer drive and park in my spot off the alley. And if the workmen are there with their van, make them move."

"Workmen? Do I know them?"

"How should I know?" Pure Stephanie. But the possibility that workmen might be there—that I might see—that might, might, *might* see Tyler…who might just possibly have quit messenger work to go back to carpentry was enough to get me downstairs, through the shop, the kitchen, and—it wasn't easy —out the side door.

I moved purposefully but not quickly. Astounded to find myself in a zone of calm. With only a few people dotting the street, I automatically raised my fingers in a catchall blessing as they approached. One woman stopped to exclaim, "Joy and Peace!" "Love and Happiness!"

And I answered "Oh Happy Day!" and "Same to You!"

What *had* I been dreading?

And then for a few minutes I was out under a low, obscured sun—alone. No cars or pedestrians. The sky, the street, and buildings were uniformly cold and gray. I stopped on the corner, arrested by an evanescent scent of evergreens and sturdy marigolds between pockets of dog shit and gasoline. It was so amazing to watch a flock of geese in the sky. And the trees! Ribbons of yellow and gold appeared strewn through the stark canopies of bare black branches. Dead leaves rushed over my feet. I raised my face in front of a towering conifer and green needles blazed red against the crazed black of my eyelids. Here I was a natural creature but also—no one was looking; I spread my arms—*supernatural*: There was, for a heartbeat, no doubt.

*

Inside the RWR garage, a short, plump, wispy-haired woman in brown coveralls hurried out from a glass booth, saying, "Well, hello there!" She wiped her hands on a rag. "I'm Amanda Rittner, but of course you know that already, don't you?"

I shook her hand and a swatch of mottled red flared up her neck. Clasping that hand to her bosom, she asked if I preferred the Lexus or the Range Rover. "I'm afraid we've sold the others." She turned her head and hiccupped into her collar.

Eyes brimming, she whispered, "Please forgive me. It's just that I've wanted to meet you for so long…"

"Oh." Embarrassed, I decided the polite thing to do was to change the subject. "Um," I pulled my chin. "Do we still have the white station wagon?"

"You mean the Chevy Carlos *gave me*? Oh God! I didn't say that. Yes. Of course, we have it. It's around back. I'll pull it up for you."

"No. No, that's all right."

But she was gone. I shifted my weight until a horn blared and the door rose, and there was my rattly old car, engine running. Except it was hers. So I shook my head no. "No, that's all right; I was just curious."

"Now, now," Amanda Rittner was holding the driver's door open, "I insist." And Lord, God, how I wanted to jump in and drive away! Who was Carlos to give away *my* car? And yet I really shouldn't make off with the ride this woman depended on. But before I knew it, I was already behind the wheel, strapped in, the time-worn seat molded to my form. I had WBMX on the box, my elbows out, I was home. "Tell Carlos I said you can have either of the other cars."

"Okay."

"I mean for keeps."

She checked my expression, no fooling, then broke into joy. "Wait," she called, pulling a small pad of paper from her pocket. "Write it down."

"Which do you want? Or, why be petty? You can have both."

"No, no," she said, her whole body shaking. "Just the Range Rover."

I jotted down the terms and signed my name. "Tell Carlos I'll thrash it out with him later, along with a few other things." And off I drove, feeling solemn and absurd. ≈

Solemn and Absurd (2)

November 13

I don't know what I expected. For so long I've run through the same moves in the same place: And now! Myriad rays bouncing in all directions. Buildings, roads, regular people going through their regular paces—it's as if I never left.

The car's like a boat and I'm gliding along. The steering wheel's loose in my hands. Jazz on the radio, Northwestern on my right, up ahead, all around. It's as if all I have to do is cut over behind the library, park—*this car was new then*—and Colin and I will find each other in the glass library on the fourth floor. Colin's slumped in the leather chair looking out on the deserted beach, black waves pounding the rocks. He's feverish and jittery, sunk in his huge stiff green army coat, watch cap on his head. And brazenly smoking, risking electronic alarms and a semester's expulsion, his cupped hand an ashtray. His legs swing up and around as I hop off the elevator. Gravity lets go. We drift, we float to each other, foreheads touching, and knees. He pinches his cigarette out and drops it in his pocket. We rise off the ground, his arms around me. He doesn't care who sees. With him and me, rules don't count. We want the same things and dream the same dreams. And oh—it was supposed to last forever. But:

Even though time didn't matter, we still would have aged. Colin and I would have changed from the boys we were. Unless, *unless*—it hits me and I hit the brakes just as the traffic lights on Sheridan Road all turn green at once. But of course:

> *I was supposed to go with him!* He spun me and I spun him, and—what was I thinking? I let instinct override faith. Some part of me interfered—I stopped short of the edge but without thinking. *Until now.*

Horns and sirens all around. If the Chevy ever had an air bag, it was stolen long ago. So I'm out of the car, and trying to comfort the tearful, unwieldy young woman who hit me. Her pure, creamy, abundant skin is magnificent. But when a cop pulls up on a motorcycle and she lowers her head, her scalp appears red and itchy through dozens of carefully plastered-down hairs. A perspective that readies me to sign over whatever I have remaining to her. If I have anything remaining.

She hit you from behind, the cop says. But I say, no, no, I was at fault. I wasn't looking. Write me a ticket.

Five, ten minutes of rigmarole. Twenty-four-year-old Amberly Severnson sobs the whole time, her angel's complexion blotching beneath streams of tears. I hand her a deposit check with my name, address, and phone number. And she gasps. "You're him! You're *him!*"

The cop says, "Who?"

And Amberly Severnson jumps in the air, elated, "The prophet, the leader, Religion Without Rules!" as I'm finally, numbly driving away.

Eventually, I pull right onto Belden. Then left again, down a few blocks to an alley with a ramshackle garage. A light shines from the square yellow brick building. What am I doing again? Oh that's right: carpenters and aquariums. I'm here to recapture the promise of my youth; to revise a pact—"Not even death is irredeemable!"—with my long-lost lover. *And* I am here to impress the beautiful boy-apprentice with a wealth of untapped beauty of my own.

But no one's here. The outside of the building has high semi-circular stained glass windows, half suns bobbing in whirls of blue. Inside, I'm far from convinced Stephanie and Rafe even lived here. Only two aquariums are stocked with fish, the rest just water and plants. The tanks glow with internal light. The hum of bubbling filters adds to the claustrophobic air. Otherwise, the space suggests a suite of vacated offices. Boxes here and there, commercial carpeting, fat cables poling out of raw holes.

The place is spectral; the artificial light and fantastical creatures sealed inside the walls scare me. The fish and corals, anemones, whatever they're called, zip back and forth or undulate in place. Some are bigger than my head. And their colors are electric: blue, yellow, magenta and orange. Some have no trace of anything resembling eyes or mouths, others the opposite: fat purple lips and big sly eyes ringed in black, or else, great fleshy knobs for lids and gaping whiskery maws.

I jump when the phone rings. "Hello?"

There's a pause on the other end. A familiar voice starts to say one thing but switches to, "Malkie? Don't hang up. Stephanie told me where you were and it's too hard to talk to you face to face right now!"

I slam the receiver down, trying to quell the anger and injury swamping my blood.

The phone's on voice mail and I'm thinking, "Fuck her," when I decide to tell her off.

"Malc—" She must be able to cry at will.

"Maggie, I have nothing to say to you. Zero interest in anything you say or do, ever, ever again."

"Malkie, *I'm sorry!* You've no idea. And oh God, it's not like you *really* need me. Carlos just wants you to think you do."

What is it with me? All Maggie has to do is cry into the phone; and I cave.

She left me alone with Carlos and the whole goddamn collapsing cult. And so how do I answer the tearful little traitor? "That's okay, Maggie."

"No," she sobs. "It's not okay. It was stupid of me, and horrible. And there's a lot of stuff I need to tell you. Mostly about money."

"Maggie, I can't do it anymore. I want out. Just like Stephanie."

"Stephanie's not getting out. Everything's going to be okay."

"You and Carlos can have everything. All I want is one store. Stephanie's getting the Lincoln Park store, and I'll take whichever one you and Carlos say."

"You know we're about to default on five loans." Maggie says. "No one is going to let you off with just one store, Malcolm!"

A visceral jerk and I revert to playground bravado. "Well, then," my voice jumps unconvincingly, "first, it's declare bankruptcy and then I guess, plastic surgery."

"You can't get out of this, Malcolm—you *are* it. Religion Without Rules is under some big, *big* debt. Personally, I think we should pull back on the nightly meetings and build up pay-TV events. Step up the merchandising. As well as give back every give-back we can come up with."

"Maggie, I really don't think I can do it another day."

"Yes, you can, Malcolm! Hang in there."

"What about you?" I ask her. "Are you hanging in?"

"Um, we'll have to talk about that. But...hey, do you want to have lunch with Tyler and me?"

"Oh, that's right. You have his number."

"He's just a boy," Maggie says. "Calm down, come home, and meet him."

"No." ≈

A Collapsing Cult

November 22

Thanksgiving. Maggie's slaving away in the kitchen, making a traditional meal for one happy little family: her, Carlos, Louie, Demetria, and me—and Ted and Janice, who are going to start videotaping me 'round the clock. "Right footage, right production and release," Carlos says heartily, "and our troubles are over."

"Troubles? What troubles?" I am perfectly tranquil. "How can people as enlightened as us have troubles?"

"Well, not troubles," Carlos concedes. "Expenses, let's say."

"A drop in the ocean."

"That's right," Carlos says. "That's exactly right." The acolytes and devotees have the day off to prepare for a big meeting tonight. Carlos wants them to milk the crowd really hard: *Pry* those wallets open. He's got a guy training them. And you know what? I don't care! The meetings mean nothing to me anymore. I stand up, say whatever pops to mind, make a little show of swaying and sweating, and that's it. Why was I ever so petrified? What was the big deal?

"Yes. Hello." "Look to your neighbor." "Wish no one ill will." I had problems saying that? No sensible person expects me to fix his situation. Press the flesh, offer a few bromides— that's all anybody wants.

*

Ted and Janice are setting up to shoot part of their infor- mercial. And they can't get over the change in my appearance.

"How much weight have you lost?" Ted asks so gravely I take it as disapproval.

But as Janice focuses her camera on a tripod, she says, "You look great. This should run half an hour and it's going to be smashing."

Smashing? I don't even flinch. Call it what they will.

Carlos lifts a lock of my hair to say, "Beauty corrupts."

And looking directly at him, I think: *You have no power over me.*

From the kitchen comes a crash, a scream, another crash, and a sustained wail. Maggie's splayed on the floor, crying over a mess of pumpkin mix, a broken plate, and a torn tent of dough. I pull her up and smooth back her hair. "Maggie, why are you doing this, and not Carlos?" She's sobbing and hiccupping. "It's not just the pie. The turkey's been in the oven forever and nothing's happening." There are chopped bits of celery and onion all over the floor, and knives and pots and pans scattered over the countertop.

I check the oven with the turkey in it and find she's set the timer but not the temperature. "Maggie, how many turkeys have you cooked in your life?"

"Like Wendy in Peter Pan," she sobs, "I *liked* playing the mother." ≈

Didn't We

Carlos tells me because Maggie claims she can't. She's moving in two weeks. To California.

Stephanie's already gone.

How much cash, Carlos wonders, do I think I can I rake in a week? "If you pull out all the stops. Half a million? A hundred thousand overnight?"

"Well, hey," I say, "if it's not impossible, why bother?"

And why not? In the face of Maggie's defection, let the record show, I am trying to bring in quick cash. I've kneaded bread at every shop, several times a day, followed by the éclair ritual, where everyone partakes; everyone smacks his lips.

Jesus, it sounds stupid. But then I realize that's the thing— I have to get past caring whether I come across stupid or ugly. I have to rise above worrying about my personal purity, my motives, my own precious stinking soul. Right? I have to go on out there and do it. Because remember—it's the reason I was born. *But shit. I just can't make that leap.* Go on out there and start a religion. Go on out there and blow millions of dollars!

And now, try to keep a straight face long enough to suck a few million back in! ≈

Fear and Desire Propel
My Heart and Mind

November 26

Maggie's moving to California in ten days. Decency alone would demand we face each other and admit together that this is the end of our friendship. Henceforth, it's a Christmas card; a maudlin, late-night phone call that I'll regret before we hang up, providing she even picks up. But Maggie is simply, always in too terrible a hurry to talk to me.

When we're perceptible to each other, in the same time and place with a mob, I telegraph, "How can you?" She tosses her head and averts her eyes. And later, when she's rushing off with other people, Maggie offers me a quickie charade. She isn't getting *out*, her fingers tiptoe. She's merely—hands in flight—moving *away*.

Several times she tells people, with me in earshot, "Turns out I can get my degree in social work inside a year…I'm already enrolled for March."

Knowing that I know that much, she will later grab my wrist even as she flees. "Omigosh, Malkie. We've got to get some time together. Don't we? We've got to."

Alone day and night, surrounded by others or not, the moment I let down my guard I slide into dream conversations with her, recalling little scenes:

> *When you first arrived from the airport, bounding up the stairs, calling "Malkie! Oh, Malkie!" an ancient cowardliness came over me. For no reason I could understand, I dived behind the drapes. And through the scrim I saw you hesitate at the threshold. I heard you cough and say, "Hello, hello." In the middle of the room you became tentative, touching the ends of your hair, turning in a circle. Did you notice my feet behind the curtains? Were you more embarrassed for yourself or for me?*

Today I found her staring out the window. Go, I ordered myself, say something to her. What's the worst that can happen? I swung toward her. My hand rose in the air. But Christ! I couldn't speak.

Afterward, I realized that for all our days and nights together, I don't know Maggie, not really. While she *does* know me. Maggie absolutely knows my every inkling—I spilled all the goods into her warm lap. She knows about Tyler, and I'm scared to death that since she's leaving, she will hold him out as compensation. She can arrange lunch. What if I just don't have it in me to resist?

She'll say, "Let me set something up." And I'll protest. "No, please don't."

But she won't be fooled. She knows how desperately I *don't* want it but *do* want it. I'm terrified of seeing him and dying to see him. She knows how fear and desire propel my heart and mind, and I all but kill myself to bring them under control. ≈

With Wolves at the Door

All at once, banks are calling! (Actually, they've been calling for months, without me knowing it. Or, more precisely, without me knowing beyond doubt.) But now—no percentage in Carlos hiding it anymore, no point in me pretending imperturbable faith—they're claiming *ownership!*

"It's not as bad as it sounds," Carlos tries to explain. "I was going to lay out the sequence for you in a few days, when, believe me, the terms will be much improved. In fact, with any luck, they could turn out for the best." His jasmine-scented hand presses my shoulder. What a shame I even had to hear of this unfortunate but fleeting misapprehension, let alone hear it from the lawyers' lawyer. (It turns out the Brazil twins, Fletcher and Franklin, are suing us.)

When the news first registered, I collapsed on the green and white settee in the main atrium. What was wrong with me that I had let my business run to ruin? I used to be so careful calculating expenses, debt, loans, and collateral. The last time I tallied the books, there was one shop and it was mine alone.

And even then I had misgivings! Remember? There were discrepancies. Yet instead of resolving them, I must have vacated my body, letting aliens take over! How else to explain it? You'd think I *wanted* to be bankrupt!

But for all my shock, I can't shake this little voice insisting that of course I knew all along—I saw the handwriting everywhere. Carlos would say, "We're overextended," and I'd shrug, "Oh well." He'd ask if I could pull in ten thousand a show, and I'd say, "Gee, what do you think?"

I couldn't give up on a primary, nameless belief. More than anything I longed to believe that Carlos—what? *Loved me?* As much as I should have known, as much as I *did* know: Carlos couldn't love anyone—especially not me! But I was stupid, stupidly determined: As long as I worked at it constantly—it would happen. Given my will and my perseverance, the day would come when Carlos would finally see he could not live without me! (Egotistical as hell and naive as a newborn, but I *did* believe. I *was* sincere.)

And so, as suppliers threatened and our stock of cars and computers dwindled, and accounting mishaps screamed disaster, I shrouded myself in unshakable conviction. For whether or not he loves me, there *is* something major between us. Right?

In the atrium, staring into my eyes, he says, "It's you and me now. No one else."

He presses me down on the undersized couch, grips my shoulders, unbuttons my shirt. We're kissing and rocking, and oh God, Carlos is good. We're alone in the atrium and night has fallen. It's cold and dark outside and we're alone in the world. We're here together, warm and sweet and surging with life.

No one takes me out of myself like Carlos. I'm all soul. I'm eternal love. Until—until, well, eventually I do drift back, tenderly if briefly fulfilled. We rest and dream, our breath in sync. For the life of me, I cannot remember: *What else matters?*

≈

Me and My Manipulator

Real time, real life, real debt: those things don't disappear. Sex, love, even prayer have zero impact on financial ruin. But what can I do? I love Carlos and hate him—and cannot leave him alone. I mean: long before Religion Without Rules, I understood he was dangerous, and basically cruel. And if pressed, I'd probably admit: that was part of his allure: I have a thing for bad boys. But never once, never in all the world, did it occur to me Carlos was *an idiot!* That for all his miracles with sugar and flour, and his clever, relentless manipulation of people—he was nonetheless *as stupid as they come!*

Yes, it crossed my mind that beneath his very convincing monastic mask, Carlos was secretly profligate. And no, I never trusted him. But from that first "open mike night," Carlos assumed behind-the-scenes control so perfectly he seemed entitled, even destined, for the role.

But *oh ho* was I wrong! Builders and brokers, lawyers and consultants are calling from all corners. And Carlos is shaking, eyes glistening. He's bobbing on the edge of ecstatic and hysterical. And for once, I have no doubt, he is not acting. "Malcolm, oh, Malcolm," he clasps my hands, "we are converging on new terrain!" His tongue slides along his lips. "The good news," he says at high pitch, "is that we're operating on a whole new level."

"And the bad news?"

"There is no bad news," Carlos says. And as I'm standing there, a stippled yellow green shadow floats over his face, the transparent flag of an ageless injury. And oh man, am I a soft touch! All I have to see is the flutter of hurt in Carlos, and I want to kiss it and make it better. I want to take him in my arms and tell him, "It's okay, Big Daddy. We'll work it out."

I manage, however, to resist. My hand flips up and down. Outside, the shrieking El, a stalled garbage truck, and a rowdy cotillion of school kids are muffled by our windows and insulation. Inside, we get mostly the nullifying hum of electronics, the suppressed wishes and worries of different voices, real, imagined, and recorded. Does he love me now? He needs me, that's for sure.

Oh, for God's sake give it up already—why do I care? It's over, it's over, a thousand times over.

"Isn't it," I ask, "time to declare bankruptcy?"

"I'm still hoping the banks will give us some leeway. In fact I'm highly optimistic."

"Is it too late to declare bankruptcy?"

"In a few weeks," Carlos says, "it will be completely unnecessary." ≈

The Paragon of Level-Headedness

Maggie is leaving in three days, but she says, "Don't for a second think I won't stay totally, totally involved." She taps her chest and purses her mouth in a *please-oh-please* expression. "You know I believe in you, Malcolm."

I glance at her sidelong. "Has the day finally come? I'm 'Malkie' no more?"

She grins and gives me a little shove. "It's not my fault you're so cute."

Hurt and baffled as I am, where would I be without Maggie? Why, even as she's packing her bags, she intervenes on my behalf, insisting to Carlos he lighten my schedule. Too many meetings, with suddenly small, touristy audiences. Religion Without Rules, I'm afraid, is fast becoming a curiosity. Last night there were only about twenty people. Mostly dentists was my impression; dentists who'd come from an association dinner at the Hyatt.

"Give him a break," Maggie says. "Concentrate on videos

and Doctrine signings. The meetings are worse than a crap shoot and they take a terrible toll."

Carlos's voice is flat and fragile. "Well, we must do something."

"We will," Maggie says. "We are. Things will pick up."

"Easy for you to say," Carlos says, "as you run off to get your fucking CSW or whatever it is in California."

"I'm not running off. I'm just going there, to learn."

"Whatever you say, Maggie. Far be it from me," Carlos says, "to doubt your commitment. To say nothing of your integrity."

"Fuck you, Carlos." (This is me talking.)

"The three days until you leave," I tell Maggie, "are starting to feel like a long, long time."

"To me, too," she says. "I'm sorry."

To which I answer, "Sorry, sorry, sorry, that's your mantra. Well, I don't care anymore."

"Don't say that," Maggie's at my side, her voice soft, her arm around my waist. "What's the worst that can happen?"

"Exactly. What have *I* got to lose?"

"I mean," Maggie says, "see this through."

"No." And this is fun—I turn and walk away. As if it were that simple.

"You won't get anywhere," Maggie says as I reach the threshold.

And, much as I hate to, I stop to hear what else she has to say. Because for all my righteousness, I don't know where I'm going. My plan is just to walk and keep walking.

"You'll still be you," Maggie says, "and for a long time everyone who sees or hears or knows of you, will recognize you."

In bewilderment, I shake my head. "So it's like I'm trapped?"

"It's like that for everybody," she says.

Which can't be true, but never mind.

Carlos butts in: "Don't put so much pressure on yourself, Malcolm."

And I laugh.

"Me? You think *I'm* doing it, Carlos? You're the one that's got me looking at bankruptcy! And probably tax evasion. *'I know what I'm doing, Malcolm. I've wanted this all my life.'* You know shit!"

A paragon of level-headedness, he says, "I was thinking of that time you went silent on stage. And since now we're scrambling, if that happens again, simply sustain it. Stand there and let it build. Don't run out like last time."

"Don't run out," Maggie says. "And remember to smile." (She steps aside to mug this last bit.) And I search the air: *abracadabra, anger disperse!* Maggie can kid all she wants, she's leaving.

Carlos and I are stuck with each other. I feel like that archetypal guy dragging himself through the desert in search of water. There's no turning back, no end in sight. ≈

In Any Furious Moment

December 15

He really gambled on the stock market. Managing or should I say *mis*managing our wildly fluctuating portfolio with the help of Herb Plochman (a broker, not an accountant; that was one of Carlos's countless little lies), we took out second and third mortgages on four different properties. Besides our six up-and-running bakeries, we're in arrears for twelve very expensive vacant places. The computers and cars, bakery and restaurant equipment, residential and commercial furnishings, Carlos bought with an appalling cascade of small business loans. Salaries he paid in cash, which makes me worry about the tax arrangements. In September, when the stock market took another downturn and the Linden Street store was opening, he consolidated with a *ten million dollar loan* Fletcher and Franklin helped him get from Bank of America. Then, with his plan to "go national" he decided to try taking the enterprise public. He sent Maggie off to California, and got Fletcher and Franklin talking to Credit Suisse to plan a stock offering. After a little digging, of course, Credit Suisse backed out. So we've been floating on infomercials and T-shirts, meetings, and music videos since October, but now it's collapsing pretty fast. We've maxed out a 52-card deck of Visas, MasterCards, Discovers, and Optimas.

Which is so pathetic and predictable, I can't stand it! Once I realized how bad it was, I had no choice but to call my parents. Two or three times a day now I have to deal with Mom and Pop on conference calls, my raw anxiety bringing on false but terrible heart attacks. I die a thousand times a day. And not even my parents' big bucks can bail me out this time. It's too far gone. My father's hired a law firm—Simon, Wagner, Gifford, and Dorman—but my prospects are far from pretty. When I first wake up in the morning, rising from at best a grainy semi-consciousness, jail, it seems, would be a relief.

"You're not going to jail over a run-of-the-mill bankruptcy and a couple of tax mistakes," Carlos says. "It's not like you're Al Capone."

"If you say so."

And though it's nuts, because we're in desperate straits, we end up giggling. He's still saying, "Do more meetings. Make more videos. Push the merchandise. And above all—*have faith!*" And we're so disoriented, everything blends into its opposite. Love, hate, light, dark, are all the same. Disaster is amusing. Life and death are equally gruesome and sublime, and in any furious moment, so real, they're surreal. Twice today when Carlos staggered in to moan, "This is awful, terrible, disastrous!" I sputtered and he snickered. And then we howled together over the next inevitable remark, which we both made in fits of tears and laughter. "Hey, it's not funny!" ≈

No Eye Contact, Please

Maggie's plane leaves in three hours, and a car is picking her up. For us, no awkward hugs in front of the metal detectors at O'Hare. Instead, I wait in the sun room like someone about to undergo day-long tests at the doctor's. I play with this and that on my phone, and wonder if I'll ever climb the Himalayas. A line of thought as grandiose as it is tenuous. Or wait—maybe not. Who's to say I can't enroll in rock climbing school once I flail out of this financial mess? I can hire a guide, join an expedition. I can begin again.

Speaking of which, here she comes. Maggie and I are still locked in our same little game of chicken: who's going to say good-bye first? She plunks herself beside me with a teasing sing-song.

"Hey, sweetie, want to go on a walk?"

"Why?"

"Because that way we can walk and talk together without feeling awkward about looking or not looking at each other."

"Okay."

"And," she babbles on, "just being outside is kind of an improvement. Natural surroundings, wider perspective."

"Sounds like you've thought this through." Basically, it's been my plan to shake Maggie's hand and part with a businesslike, "Best of luck."

But she stands up half-bowing. Her face and posture, her whole demeanor beseech me. "It doesn't have to be a long walk," she says. "Around the block."

My face burns and I stare at my shoes.

"Malcolm, you know I believe in you, and your spirituality."

Disgusted, I practically spit. But uh-oh! Her eyes are misting up; her hands are twisting, knuckle over knuckle. And I am pure jellyfish. My arm around her, I'm up and cooing, "Of course I'll go on a walk with you."

"Wait." She's snuffling and wiping her cheeks. "Carlos is getting someone to take my place, and it won't be easy for you."

"Maggie, isn't there enough going on? We're supposed to be saying good-bye."

"Jesus, I know that! It's just—well, you acted so weird about Tyler's cell phone and got so panicky when I said, 'Why don't the three of us have lunch?'"

"Oh," I stagger back.

"I tried to talk Carlos out of it."

"Whatever you do, Maggie, don't tell me anymore about this."

"Okay."

And though it's midday, there's a twilight cast in the room, ephemeral specks of silvery dust. There's a strangeness at hand, a dull and staticky foreboding. Maggie sighs: "It's just too much. You and Carlos are going to have to do whatever it is you need to do, make up, break up, start over—without me in the middle."

"Maggie, if that's why you're moving to LA, don't go. And don't go thinking you'll do conferences there. We've got about a week, a month at the most, before the banks shut us down."

"Don't say that."

"It's true." And ambling beside her in the stark, gray, completely uncontrollable atmosphere outside, I latch on to this *she-done-me-wrong* scenario. As if Maggie were leaving me for some younger, sexier, holier holy man. I brood, my bottom lip out. *You'll be sorry someday.* She cocks her head, flashing me a wicked smile. *And you'll have hell to pay.* I stamp my feet, kick the curb. We should write a song.

*

For half an hour, we stroll along, two ordinary friends on an ordinary afternoon. Maggie points to a flock of crows tottering on someone's lawn. We're scuffling through a carpet of dead leaves when a little girl skates by, holding a sheet cake with a big 9-shaped candle stuck in the frosting. "'Scuse me," she says, gliding past. We watch the swing of her beaded African braids, her long legs, and the fluttering back of her velvet coat as she disappears around a corner.

We cross back on Sheridan Road and a high-speed cyclist,

all muscle and Lycra, spokes, gears, plastic and chrome, spins past us. He or she rips right into the horizon, so it seems *we're* a blur.

We cut through the plaza of candy and jewelry stores. A man in headphones coming from the other end is waving a phantom baton. Upon noticing us, he freezes, then decides—you can see his mind working—to resume his fantasy, a notch lower in volume and velocity. Up close the would-be conductor's face is red and wet.

"He doesn't look so good," Maggie says as we approach a stone entranceway.

"No," I agree. We emerge through the plaza's entry arch. We round a corner of wrought iron fence, slip past a tremendous pine tree, and then, just like that, it's happened: We're on our way back.

With the window boxes of home in view, Maggie turns sideways and grabs my wrists—shouting: "About my replacement: Whatever your problem is, you'll handle it."

"It's funny you should say that." I lunge to keep up with her.

Her hands describe a horizontal plane as she says in wry amazement, "It's just so much work being out in broad daylight. It's like you have to incorporate yourself into the world." Tossing her hair from her eyes, she grins. "I sound just like you."

I'm all set to protest, *Hey, come on, that's not what I sound like*; when an unsettling clamminess creeps over her face. Her expression flattens and off her skin comes an oily chill.

I shade my eyes, trying to see what she's seen. Through the

plate-glass window Carlos is blocking someone from view. Vaguely lithe and long-haired is my impression. Of course, I know it's Tyler, but I won't admit it. It's nothing. Why sweat? It's nothing.

Then Maggie pounds me in the small of my back. She shoves me ahead of her, and runs on my heels, forcing me ahead. After half a block it occurs to me to refuse, and I stop dead.

"What?"

"It's no excuse, but—" She takes my arm and proceeds farther down the street. "But God—why do we only get impossible choices? It may seem like I'm running out on you, Malcolm, but I'm really not. It's going to be fine." Maggie's hurrying backwards, away from me. "You're going to discover it's much, much simpler than you thought."

"*What* is?"

Maggie looks over her shoulder, "I know you won't hurt him. You'll see."

And she runs to a two-tone, beige and tan, Seventies model Mercedes, which I hadn't noticed until now, has been cruising behind us for several minutes. She's calling, "I believe in you, Malkie! I love you!" And I'm aware of a driver leaning over to open the passenger's door. Maggie's crying and waving good-bye, don't worry, it's all going to turn out all right. She's sure; she believes; she has complete faith. And then the car pulls away and she's gone. ≈

I Remember

December 18

After that, my recollection produces a wispy haze and few signs of life. I know I ambled for hours, in the dark, during the day, as if in shock. If I treaded on grass or asphalt, beneath trees or birds, above worms and bugs; if, in transit, I passed people on limb-flapping power walks, crossing guards, school kids—nothing penetrated.

I remember feeling suspended, adrift, as if my soul were holding its breath. My goal was to keep moving. Please God, let a path form, a door open, as long as I stay on my feet. If I act natural…If I behave scrupulously, a clean and perfect way out might—might—appear out of nowhere.

As Maggie's adieus ebbed into history, a crest of admonitions—*don't worry, never fear*—buoyed me along. Hopping from foot to foot, I decided my existence is not marginal, as I've always feared; it's grotesque! It's glaring and conspicuous! There's no disguising what a bulbous, quivery thing I am.

*

At the intersection of Green Bay Road and Maple, a show-off-y couple (mink coats, silver Mercedes) blatantly ran a red light. The driver behind them, inching forward in a Dodge plastered with Jesus stickers, was singing Christmas Carols at the top of his lungs. Hands on the steering wheel, head back, mouth open, his chest was heaving, his eyes shut. As the light changed, a cigarette-smoking young woman behind him leaned on her horn, making me jump. A simultaneous gust of cold lashed at my skin. I felt it pierce my bones, and on the outside, push me, so that I stumbled and shuddered and oh, I don't know: This business of us each being separate creatures struck me as nonstop neediness, no matter what.

I crossed onto Washington Avenue, away from the wind, toward, I hoped, normalcy with its little shops and single-family homes. For a while I encountered no one. Then a blotchy-faced man in winter coveralls lurched—drunkenly—from a pink gravel driveway. With a can of Budweiser in one hand and a rock in the other, he headed straight for me. I was backing away, but he begged, "No, come on, wait. Take a look at this." He turned over the rock, revealing a dazzling purple and white geode the size of a half-grapefruit. "Go on," he said, "take it."

"No, but thank you."

"I want you to have it, achu-ally." He swiped at my shoulder. "Because achu-ally, it much more belongs to you than to me."

Assuming he wanted money, I slapped my pockets. "All I've got is a twenty."

"Will you fuck that? What do you think I am? A fucking door-to-door lucky rock salesman? Don't you know you are looking at your biggest, truest, hard-fucking-est-core believer on the planet?"

Not facetiously (at least at the time, it didn't sound as bad to me as it does here), I said, "You do look familiar."

"Take the rock."

"Thank you." And upon inspecting the geode, I mumbled further appreciation.

My biggest hardest-core believer on the planet drained his beer, tossed the empty can in some bushes, and said, "Now give me your blessing."

I cleared my throat and was about to resort to a tap on the cheek and a *Dominus Nabisco*, when the man ranted instructions at me. "Touch my head," was all I could clearly make out. So, "Here, hold this—" I handed him back the geode and stroked wiry tufts of his mustard-brown hair. For good measure, I pressed my thumbs against his temples. *Go*, I thought of saying, *and drink no more*. But that seemed pretentious, even for me.

Instead, I asked, "What can I do for you?"

My rock-giver bowed his head, saying "Keep me steadfast in love," as I mentally sifted through nostrums: *Okay, sure. Go on and be steadfast.*

"And," continued the drunk, "keep me forever in awe of your holiness."

What can you say to that?

I said, "Go. And drink no more."

*

Then I turned and ran, ending up in a grove of birch trees between Northwestern and the beach. Something about the low invisible sun, the stark white branches and the imperceptibly changing sky cut a gash of desperate grief in me. Shadows shifted and I realized that Colin and I in our brief, hectic comings and goings had come here. More than once. Or else the one time seemed like many. We'd taken turns pressing each other up against the slender, white-barked trees, me on him, him on me. It was a game; there was a rhythm: first be serious, for real, the lover and his beloved.

Pinning my beloved to a tree, I clasped his two wrists in my one hand, and stared into his infinitely deep-lit eyes, half-stunned, half-searching: Where was Colin? In there? In me? And then, mystified, I leaned back and noticed his mouth, which as soon as I saw it, I had to have. We kissed and laughed at how stupid we were being. Should we run back and do it again? Why not?

> You can set it up anyway you want. Whatever it is that happens to everyone else would never happen to us! Colin and I were incorruptible.
> We didn't know.
> We took turns playing lovers among these trees. We stood motionless in the snow. Ice glinted from every twig but we were not cold. We were extraordinarily alive! in love! And if somehow I got stuck as lover and he as beloved, why even keep track?

Now you be me and I'll be you.

So why is it, when the one thing you've always wanted finally appears—it's here, it's yours—it's already practically gone? Love in the birch grove was that kind of turn. A beginning and an end—which I was aware of even as it happened. It was like: Let me remember this, give me a second to fix it in place, because this is where I'm going to live my life from here on. *Memorize this so you can come back.*

And now, I had—come back. Accidentally, all these years later. Overhead a caw, a creaking bough, something made me look up. *If only I had known then...*And here, my mind stuck. Since I had known enough to isolate, and savor, and commit to memory what every minute being with him was like. I had had premonitions all along that being in love with Colin was too good to be true. Terrible, unexplainable twinges and ominous inklings that everything changes; nothing lasts.

*

Shivering in this isolated birch grove, I'm blind for a second until I discover I've shut my eyes, that's all. Head back, I stretch and spin, competing with the treetops. We're jockeying for position beneath shimmery banks of clouds. And then... here it comes—I start to see what's been in the offing all day.

Carlos has that boy in his clutches! Please God, help me rescue this perfectly innocent boy from evil. I mean: Let me resist the thrall of his beauty and that deep, high and low swing as I recognize in him the soul of concern, of sweetness, light, peace, joy and hope! ≈

One Hundred Percent Used-to-Be

December 19

Expecting to collapse any second, I burst through walls and plunge through black holes. Finally, in the shadow of the garage across the street, I bend to catch my breath. In a minute I will storm the compound. I'll hoist the boy over my shoulders and race him to safety...

*

The frightening thing is how suddenly, perfectly easy it is. I saunter through the massive shop—no boy in sight!

Gamely, I pat a stolid man's shoulder. "Yes, hello! It's so good to see you." He's eating a sticky pecan roll and his beleaguered face with its puffed, almost shut eyes elicits more tenderness than despair. Not that I'm not despairing: Who knows what's ahead? And what Carlos is capable of?

But the stolid, dejected man stops chewing. And I say, "Hang in there. It will be okay." We exchange honest, timid smiles—that's all he wants—and I'm on to the next one.

A pale, thin woman in a corduroy dress jumps up and extends her hand. There's a flicker of sprightliness behind a pre-assembled expression. Her real smile is shaky. "We need to have *faith*," she says.

"No, no. We're supposed to doubt." For once I'm sticking to the premise. "Faith and doubt go hand in hand." And like an amnesiac come to his senses, I say the words and shudder with revelation; how long had I blanked on Religion Without Rules's central tenet?

"Okay," She tugs at her reddish, helmet-like hair. "I'll grant you that—"

"Thank you." A bubble, a tickle, a nice, normal exchange. That's how far I am from anxiety.

So why am I sick with foreboding? Why am I…Oh yes, here's the reason. Here comes Carlos, tongue wetting his lips. He hurries out from behind the long, sleek countertop. We immediately make eye contact, and—I do not flinch. Something happened back there in the birch grove. A trans-formation? A connection or communion with Colin. Tyler and Colin are not alike; I invented a connection out of nothing. To be honest, Tyler doesn't even resemble Colin. He's no longer someone I desire.

And further, how odd that someone decided he should replace Maggie as my personal assistant, someone paid to be friendly and understanding. Who decided I needed someone like that? Only Carlos would have the idea that being friendly toward me was in fact a job description. But now she's not here and if Tyler has signed on for a position, someone must tell him the position no longer exists.

Carlos and I have battled telepathically for so long that next time we find ourselves in the same room, he'll know. The next time Carlos and I are within spitting distance, he'll know: Tyler Dineen can't work here. We can't afford it. His life and career will come to him, but neither Carlos nor I will interfere. Forcing Carlos to honor my decision may require exertion. We must agree with or without discussion. For once, I'm determined to do whatever it takes.

Carlos can fuss and fume till kingdom come. No actual empire is depending on my every move. Whatever we once fantasized might be at stake has vanished, abracadabra—poof!

Carlos has been inside my head, tormenting my heart all year. He's stayed with me and, yes, in his way, as long as Maggie was there to talk me down and hold my hand in the morning, he's loved me. But now that's gone; I'm holding his gaze without flinching. Carlos ruling my body and soul is one hundred percent used-to-be. He can't hurt me! He can't touch me!

We're standing across from each other as I spell this out in my head. So he has the message. *I'm not fooling, Carlos.* Either you contact the boy or I will turn him away the day he arrives. And if I seem cruel, all right. I'll seem cruel. A liar, a fake—no one can think worse of me than I've already felt. Suffered, repented, and recovered. Once I was cruel. Now I'm not.

And Carlos inching closer to me gathers all of the above. His eyes betray his alarm. Those hang-dog big brown old-man's eyes shine with something like shock and quickly close, glance elsewhere as utter disbelief suffuses his face. Carlos clears his throat as if to try again, like pumping the gas pedal. I'm watching his mouth twist. Gently, I shake my head, like, way past time to give it up, honey, baby, muffin. Can't you see, how immeasurably far I am beyond you?

"Excuse me." I return my attention to the red-haired woman. "Before we were so rudely interrupted, I was about to say, try not to worry, but if you *do*…"

"I know! I know what you're going to say: 'Don't worry about worrying.' "

We both smile and Carlos dances around me, rubbing his hands. "Well, well, well. Lo and behold!" Determined to claim me, he drops a heavy arm upon my neck.

"The better to steer me with," I say.

"What?"

"No need to carry me off, Carlos. You honor my conditions and I'll honor yours."

"Okay, fine." He releases my shoulder, and holding up his wrongly accused hands, ushers me into the office. From here, it's like looking at a series of stills, pose after pose of Carlos in sympathy and regret. I see the one where his head dips. The one where his eyes turn up. The one where he clasps his hands. Now we're at the one where he leans in to me. I notice he's speaking and his words are at such odds with what's actually going on, I have to laugh. It's a loud sputter, and Carlos decides to indulge me.

"I realize, Malcolm, that Maggie's defection—um," he

continues solemnly, "must seem like a terrible setback. But given time, I'm sure it will turn out for the best."

"Why thank you, Carlos. Your concern touches me." Not to be unfair, I try mentally rotating his head, to see if from some other point of view I might possibly be wrong. Was there a catch in his voice just now, a telltale quiver?

Under my prolonged (and I imagine unnerving) scrutiny, Carlos says, "You know, you have a really nice profile, Malcolm."

"Flattery? You're trying flattery, Carlos?"

"I'm not 'trying' anything, Malcolm. You turn on tiptoe and stick your nose in the air. What am I supposed to say?"

"You want to know the last thing Maggie said to me? Just before she bailed? She yelled, 'Carlos's new assistant was not my idea! It's not my fault!' "

"Good-byes are tough," Carlos says. "But," he sighs, eyelids aflutter. "Life. Must. Go on. Our new assistant is a bright and very capable convert."

"We're not hiring a replacement for Maggie or in any way enlisting one. I'm a big boy now. Haven't you noticed? The idea of a baby-sitter simply won't work anymore."

"What are you talking about?"

"No new assistant. If you misspoke when you mentioned a bright and capable convert or were predicting the future, forget I said anything. But if you've actually arranged for someone to play Maggie's role, the play's changed. Fewer characters."

Carlos clears his throat, a belabored, hawking action. "However you want."

White flecks cake the corners of Carlos's lips. We're standing in the hall, and his voice is hoarse with fervor. It cracks; it trills with misery. "Please! Malcolm. Listen."

Wanting one more try, Carlos pins me to the wall and runs his hands over me.

I tap his shoulder. "You don't have to do this."

But he grinds into me, kissing my neck.

You'd think I'd relish a chance to laugh in his face, but all I feel is sorry. Stopping his efforts, I can't believe the emptiness. "Carlos, Carlos! On to Plan B."

And you know Carlos. He shrugs. "Fine. Plan B."

But of course I hope it's just me making stuff up and there is no Plan B. "Carlos, we're only in business till Monday. Then we're in bankruptcy court."

I'm asking his back. For there the boy is, sprawled in an armchair, listening to headphones. He smiles when he sees me. He jumps up, pulls the headphones down to his neck, and says, "Hi." *All sweetness and soul, all concern, pure light, peace, joy, hope, and more!* More than anyone can fathom.

And I—I'm glowing and humming, elated. He's shaking my hand. It's the most natural thing in the world. "Hi, I'm Tyler. We met before. Do you remember?"

"Yes. But—" A band of heat develops behind my eyes, and I forget to breathe. Tyler is grace and cascading hair. Dark supple eyebrows and clear, deep, radiant irises. He's so much like me when I was nineteen, almost twenty. And so not at all like Colin.

"We're going into bankruptcy. I'm sorry if we misled you.

If you ever need references, here's my card. The phone number won't change."

He tilts his head, really? I nod and he shrugs. As he saunters out, I watch his back. Such a nice kid. He'll do fine. He throws me a rueful smirk good-bye, and I don't know this, but the gesture is a straight guy's minimal disappointment; nothing but so what and who cares, a full register lower than the way I think. So it's intimation, but still. Why the fuck didn't I even wonder? Tyler Dineen likes girls. One's waiting for him at home wherever he happens to live. ≈

We Couldn't Have Held On

December 21

Was I afraid the boy might afflict me like Carlos did with his lizardy maneuvers? How stupid. No, I couldn't have supposed that. Carlos is Carlos and no one else could possibly do to me what I let him do: manipulate me until I curled into his own soft mound of modeling clay. Had Colin lived, would he have affected me as much? Would I have manipulated him? Tyler reminded me of how eager and energetic we once were. I saw him as the soul of concern, of sweetness, light, peace, joy and hope. When, of course, that's in everyone. There to be tapped or shining outright. We waste and exhaust it, and sometimes, even manage to replenish it.

If Colin miraculously appeared, unchanged from the moment we headed for the roof, would I know to stop him? I miss him and mourn him. But there was nothing I could do. I didn't know, and couldn't know.

A chill courses through me, a rippling, feathery effect. There's no voice or vision. Nothing certain, just an idea of who he'd be and what he'd look like at thirty-two. More solid, less hair, an architect whose partner is a gay rights lawyer. They live in a loft with a sleek black dog they've trained well. I'm standing here, dreaming. They listen to jazz and run marathons and when he thinks of me or I think of him, there's a sharp pull.

It didn't happen like that. But Colin and I in our shared euphoria could never have lasted. We wouldn't have forgotten each other, or ever recovered. But in life or death, through time or out of it, neither one of us could have held on. ≈

Plan B

We are, thanks to my parents, well represented legally. But bankruptcy, as Carlos has so adamantly insisted, is not an end but a beginning. He has big plans to start over, while I do not. Carlos and I are married in debt but divorced for life. We'll still stage events in auditoriums for a while. I'll still hold forth, putting in appearances at the surviving bakeries. But eventually we'll strike a deal. Carlos will get money, property, even some kind of trademark if he wants. And I'll find another baker. How hard can that be? I'll run a single simple shop and sometimes, if the spirit moves me, I will sway and speak. I will offer people my prayers, press their temples, kiss the tops of their heads, telling them not to give up, to look deeper within for the immutable truth. ≈

Faith Like Desire

It's not exactly business as usual. Takeout is brisk, considering, but the main room is quiet and the offices are empty. I intend to give the acolytes, novitiates, clerks, cashiers, *et al.* some kind of severance. This contradicts Carlos's reality.

"All we have to do," he says, "is cut back and restructure. Adopt a new name, devise a new game plan."

"Not you and me, Carlos."

When my small-business-grown-huge-then-folded is finally sold in parcels and closed; and my debts and credits and Carlos's are finally divvied in two, I will come away with this much: I will have faith like desire. Faith ever changing, taking strange, threatening shapes. Or forms so tiny and faint you have to know what to look for. But I do—I know how to find them now. And when this outlandish venture is finally over, I'm going to gather up as much faith of as many kinds as I can. I'm going to nurture and cherish them always, and once they're ready, I'm going to let them loose all over the world.

≈ ≈ ≈

About the Author

Kathleen Maher wrote *Diary of a Heretic* while she raised two children in suburban Tarrytown, New York. An excerpt from the novel reached finalist status in the inaugural Richard Hall Memorial Short Story Contest sponsored by the Lambda Literary Foundation in 2000.

She is the author of Underground Nest, a novella, and her short fiction has appeared in literary journals including *Ascent*, *Black Warrior Review*, *Confrontation*, *Cottonwood*, *Descant (TCU)*, *Gargoyle*, *Passages North*, and *The View From Here*. Her work has been short-listed in numerous contests, including The William Faulkner Society Novel Competition, Iowa School of Letters Award, and Drue Heinz Literature Prize.

Her website is kathleenmaher.net, and you can email Kathleen at Beekmanpress.kmaher@gmail.com.